Cailleach

by Louise Maskill

To Pat
Enjoy the book!
With very best
wishes,
Louise x.

Hogthorn Press

Paperback © 11 December 2023
Version: 13 January 2024
ISBN: 9798875533181

Cover design by Tom Scutt
Typeset in Word in Times New Roman

Published via KDP by
Hagthorn Press
Masson House
Market Place
Crich, Derbyshire, UK
DE4 5DD

Table of Contents

Pronunciation Notes....4
1....6
2....11
3....22
4....26
5....29
6....31
7....38
8....51
9....67
10....69
11....73
12....91
13....92
14....96
15....98
16....101
17....113
18....119
Acknowledgements....124

Pronunciation Notes

Many of the names and some words in this story are based on Irish Gaelic. However, I have played fast and loose with pronunciation in my own head and may even have made some words up, so apologies in advance to Gaelic speakers…

Aengus	ANG-gus
Aillean	AL-yan
Áine	ON-ya
Ainnir	ANN-ie
Baoth	BAH-uth
Bealtaun	BEL-torn
Brideog	bri-DOWG
Cailleach	KAL-y-ach
Cairell	KA-rel
Caoimhe	KEE-va
Caomhanach	Ca-VAN-ah
Dearbhail	DJER-val
Dubhthaigh	DU-vah
Fial	Fyawl
Floinn	Fla-EEN
Gráinne	GRAY-nah
Lynet	Lih-NET
Maoilfhinn	MAL-in
Marthe	MAR-ta
Moire	MOY-rah
Muireann	Muh-REEN
Myrddin	MER-thin
Neasa	NESS-a
Ó Bragain	O'Bragan
Ó Caiside	O'Cassidy

Ó Grádaigh	O'Grady
Ó Laoghaire	O'Leary
Ó Leannain	O'Lennon
Oimelc	EEW-milk
Oillín	Will-EEN
Ríofach	REE-uh-fakh
Ríona	Ree-OH-na
Saraid	SAHR-uh
Se'enight	SEH-night (seven nights, a week)
Tanaí	TAR-nay
Uaine	Oo-EHN-ya
Úna	OO-na

1

Where to?

I have my patch, of course – the wide-bounded lands within which I roam, the well-trodden routes across them, and the loose seasonal round from place to place – but there is still a decision to be made at every crossroads. Left or right? This hamlet, or that village? This cluster of farmsteads, or that small town?

Whichever way I turn my poor aching feet, news of my arrival travels fast through the hamlet, or the village, or the town. I find a place to wait until I am directed to my space; sometimes they give me house room, but more likely I'll be with the livestock in a barn, because most often that's the only building big enough to stand the frame. Occasionally I work outside, but – well, there are reasons why that is not a good idea. Weather is not kind to fabric, and it is much easier to contain the magic, working indoors.

And most often they're pleased to see me. Oh, yes, they all want me when I arrive, the same way they want the Sunlord to warm the earth or the Hag to guide their dead to the Otherworld. They all want my frame, my thread, my expert fingers, my skills and my magic. They want me to work with the patchwork of their lives, stitching warp to weft, pattern to plain, cotton to silk, batting to backing and top. They want me to put my sweat and blood, my years of experience, my magic to work for them, thinking that my skills can make sense from the senseless, order from the chaotic, pattern from the random.

Whoever is playing host will spread the word, and as I set up in my barn, rolling the pack containing the upright struts of the frame from my back and starting to fix them together, the women will already be trickling through the open door. Some march confidently into my space with friends or family, some sidle in alone, and a few wait outside or in their own homes until most everyone else has arrived before them. However they come, though, most will have a bundle tucked under their arm, or inside their shawl, or clutched to their chest – the product of their season's work. In some places there will only be a few of these precious bundles, but sometimes there are many; then there is disappointment later, since I only ever take on a few of the pieces that are laid hopefully before me.

They watch as I set up my frame with its rollers and struts, and by the time it is bolted together and leaning against the wall the group of women will have gathered. I learn a lot from that gathering. I see those who are anxious, and those who are joyful. I see those who are grieving, those who are in love, and those who are jealous. I see which of them have quarrelled, I see who is isolated or new to the community, and who is scared. I see where my most fruitful work will lie.

Some of them will have brought food and drink for me, hoping to buy favour with gifts. I eat with gratitude, but without prejudice; sometimes the food is poor and mean and sometimes it is rich and cloying, the taste lingering in my mouth like bad memories. Either way, to me it is simply sustenance, not currency, and no more than my due.

Lamps will be lit, stools brought in from houses and workshops, and the women will sit around talking in the flickering orange light. Occasionally I will be all but forgotten, an old woman sitting quietly on the edge of the group, bony hands curled around a mug of tea, my presence only the catalyst for this feminine gathering. Often, though, I am the centre of attention; they want news of the world beyond their narrow community. Is there war? Is there famine? Is there still a king? These weighty matters interest them, in an abstract way, but they are more immediately concerned with the small and local scandals that travel with me from village to village in the pockets of the larger ones. Who has died? Who is wed? Who has been delivered of children, and who has perished in the trying? Which wife has run off with which handsome tinker, and will her husband have her back?

Time passes in these discussions, but before long someone will clear her throat and lean down to retrieve her closely-wrapped bundle from where it has been tucked under her stool. She will be diffident, apologetic, fingers plucking at the wrapping and affecting that this is a mere afterthought, ah, no, it doesn't really matter, she almost forgot to mention it. Since you're here, Cailleach, she'll say, what do you think of this?

And she will carefully peel back the outer layers of wrapping to reveal the precious contents of her bundle. Fabric will rustle and sigh as she unfolds her season's work with exaggerated care, spreading it in a space on the floor that has been left clear seemingly by accident. She will twitch it critically, smoothing wrinkles and removing pieces of thread and lint, and then she will step back.

There will be a murmuring, a leaning forward and a soft sigh as the assembled group, the woman's friends, relations, enemies and confidantes, examine the piece of patchwork stitchery laid out before them. Some may already have seen it, been present during its making, or may even have contributed precious scraps of fabric which they now point out, nodding and smiling as they take a small piece of credit for themselves. Some may reach out to touch the work, rubbing it between their fingers and flipping it over to examine the stitching on the reverse; sometimes, if the maker is confidant in her needlework, she does not mind, but sometimes there is a sharp intake of breath, almost a hiss, and the intrusive fingers drop away.

This moment belongs to them, the circle of women. Before long another of them unrolls her bundle, and then there is an eager rush, all of them clamouring to display their work to its best advantage. Lovingly hand-worked pieces of patchwork are draped over knees, held up by friends, hung from beams or rafters. Traditional patterns are recognised and recalled, and new ones are pointed out and discussed. Intricate areas of stitching are admired, and mistakes are glossed over by friends and stored away by enemies.

The complexities of their close relationships are most apparent during this time – the soft exclamations of delight, the hugs and mutual admiration, and the undercurrents of jealousy and contempt. Again, I am almost forgotten in the susurration of fabric and female voices. I sip my tea, watching and waiting for them to notice me, to remember why they are here.

Eventually someone, maybe the first woman who displayed her work, turns to me. What do you think, then, Cailleach? she asks nervously. Anything here you can work with?

Now comes my time. I set my tea down carefully and rise slowly to my feet, ancient bones creaking and complaining. I begin to move around the room inspecting their work, commenting here and there, stroking, rubbing, peering closely and squinting from a distance. In truth I have already made my choices – often before they even unrolled their work – but they need the theatre, the show of consideration and judgement.

I return to my seat, and now there is an expectant hush in the room. I sigh, enjoying the moment despite myself and playing it out as long as I can, scanning the room one last time and looking at each piece in turn as it is offered up again for my inspection. The ritual is ancient, but then, so is my magic.

I close my eyes, pretending to consider, and the women hold their breath, expectant. Some of them smile and make tiny encouraging gestures, willing me to choose their quilt; most want me to choose their piece because they think I'll give them what they want, that their life will somehow become better, cleaner, easier, richer because of my work.

For some, however, one or two, their faces betray their anxiety. They have some understanding of the truth, perhaps because they have seen the results of my work for others; they know that my magic works in ways they cannot predict. I bring them not what they want, but what they need, or else what they deserve. Then, afterwards, they may not want me so much.

I make my choice.

2

"Oh, by the Hag's skinny arse, not again!"

Aillean sucked her finger, tasting the hot metallic tang of blood. The needle in her other hand was stained red at the tip, so she wiped it on the brown homespun fabric of her overskirt, glancing up furtively as she did so to see if her mother, busy at the stove on the other side of the room, had heard her muttered blasphemy, picked up in her father's forge. Fortunately, however, it seemed her words had been lost in the clattering and bubbling of food preparation; her mother's back remained turned, and Aillean sighed softly in relief.

Blood continued to seep from her punctured finger, the taste of iron making her grimace. With her finger still in her mouth she made a close examination of the fabric she was holding, to see if she had marked it. It wouldn't be the first time, she thought wryly; sometimes she wondered if there was more of her blood on this gods-be-damned quilt than in her own body.

There was indeed a small stain, but it was on the seam allowance on the underside of the work, so it would not show anywhere on the right side of the finished quilt. This time she had been lucky, and her mother would not have to sigh and be disappointed in her all over again.

She removed her finger from her mouth and inspected it. She could still see the tiny wound, but it was no longer bleeding, and it would soon heal. Good thing too, she thought, or I'd have more seeping holes than that pincushion.

She gripped the needle firmly between the thumb and forefinger of her right hand, determined to make a decent job of stitching together the two scraps of fabric she was holding in her left. They had slipped apart while she was tending to her injured finger; frowning with concentration she replaced one on top of the other, right sides together, and anchored the thread at one end of the seam with two tiny stitches.

Except her stitches weren't tiny; they never were. Her needlework was clumsy – everyone said so, even her father who scarcely knew one end of a needle from the other, and had no desire to do so. That's women's work, he would say when she complained to him about how her mother forced her to practice, day after day in the harsh winter sunlight, night after night by the flickering lamplight. Don't bring it to me, girl.

But she did bring it to him; she did force him to inspect her patchwork, and even he who loved her to distraction had to admit that her seamlines were crooked, her stitches were uneven, the thread somehow become lumpy and the fabric bunched up where she had pulled the stitching too tight. She often sewed pieces of fabric the wrong way up, so that the dull side showed when the seam was opened out, and her mother had forbidden her to work with any shapes except squares or rectangles because of the regularity with which she placed pieces the wrong way round, throwing an entire pattern askew.

Now, she sighed as she tried in vain to make her anchoring stitches neat and accurate. No matter how hard she concentrated, though, the needle seemed determined to come up in the wrong place, and when she did finally manage to place the stitches in the correct alignment the thread somehow contrived to tangle itself into a huge snarl behind the fabric, so that it caught and refused to pull through. She cursed under her breath as she tugged it, trying to force the ragged knots to travel smoothly.

"Oh, Aillean." Her mother's hands reached around her, lifting the work from her and gathering up the tangled threads. "This is really not your strength, is it?"

Aillean scowled. She knew that she struggled with needlework, of course she did, but having her mother point it out, day after day and night after night, didn't make it any easier. At the age of thirteen this was not the first winter her mother had tried to teach her to sew, but it was the first season she had been forced to stick at it. In previous years she had been allowed to give it up as a bad job, everyone blaming her youth for her unsuccessful attempts, but this year her mother was convinced that practice would make perfect – or at least, not disastrous.

Neither did it help that her sister Marthe, younger by one year and competitive in everything she did, appeared to be a natural, able to sew straight lines with neat regular stitches and get her corners to match up every time. Marthe was watching now out of the corner of her eye, a tiny smirk on her face as she pretended to pay full attention to her own work. With her back to their mother Aillean mouthed another obscenity she had picked up from her father's apprentice boys, and had the scant reward of seeing Marthe's face twitch and her mouth stiffen into a disapproving line.

With a few flicks and jerks her mother untangled the snarl of thread, pulled the needle through in a smooth movement and sewed a few tiny stitches along the seam line. "There. I've started it for you – you can finish it. Only a few more blocks to make, and then you can start sewing them together." Giving Aillean a hopeful pat on the shoulder she turned back to the stove.

Marthe glanced up. "I've almost done too," she said. "We'll both be able to show our quilts to the Cailleach when she comes." She smiled slyly.

Aillean stuck out her tongue and scowled again. They both knew that the chances of her quilt being finished and in a fit state to show to anyone by winter's end were slim to non-existent, but Marthe had already completed one small quilt this winter and was almost done with her second. She had inherited their mother's nimble fingers, for sure.

Whereas Aillean had inherited – what, exactly? She wasn't sure she had anything from either of her parents. Both were skilful with their hands, her father a blacksmith and her mother a seamstress, but she herself seemed to be unable to make anything except a mess. Her father was also a musician, his scarred workman's hands able to coax haunting music from the waist-harp he had inherited from his own father, and her mother could sing like one of the fairy folk themselves. Aillean, however, had long ago been advised never to raise her voice in song where others might hear, and she had once broken three strings on the harp when she had tried to play it and been forbidden to touch it again.

She had thought for a while that her skills might lie in animal husbandry, but creatures had an unhappy habit of wandering off or dying when left in her care. Plants also died no matter how carefully she tended them, food she made either burned, failed to cook properly or tasted somehow wrong, she could knock things over just by walking past them, and she could never remember even the simplest of instructions when she was asked to run errands. All in all, not being able to sew was simply the latest in a long line of things she was no good at.

She sighed and squinted at the scraps of fabric in her hands. Doggedly she stabbed down with the needle and brought the point back up through the layers of fabric as she had watched her mother do, but again, somehow it didn't come up where it should. She pulled it out and had another go, but this time was worse than the first; when she pulled the thread through the stitching described a ragged zig-zag, and she knew for a certainty that the seam would never lie flat.

That was the most irritating thing of all – she knew what she was supposed to be doing, she just couldn't make her hands actually do it. Women were supposed to be able to do this stuff without thinking about it; as a tiny child, many a winter's night she had sat with her mother and aunts, drowsing around a communal fire while their fingers flew and pieces of needlework grew under their hands. They talked, laughed, sang while they sewed, and no one ever seemed to get a knot in their thread, or sew a piece the wrong way round, or ruck up a seam, or any of the things that happened to her with infuriating regularity.

She pinched her mouth into a thin line and then sketched a weak smile, aware that Marthe was watching her. She nodded to herself as if she was pleased with her progress, but instead of continuing with her stitching she put the work down and started flipping through the pile of blocks she had already made, arranging them in front of her in different orientations and patterns.

Perversely, she enjoyed this part of making a quilt; she loved seeing the patterns emerge from the scraps, the overall design hidden until the disparate pieces were put together at the end. The finished quilt was always so much more than the sum of its parts, and when she was tiny she had loved arranging and rearranging the individual pieced blocks that her mother had stitched for some project or other. She had always been intrigued by how a set of identical blocks arranged in different ways could produce such wild variations in the final pattern.

Everyone in the family had a quilt on their bed, of course, all made by her mother or her grandmother. There was also a cedarwood chest full of extras, ready to be pressed into service when they were needed – thick ones for winter, thin ones for summer, small ones for children's beds or for tucking around the knees of the old folk. There were ancient ones, worn almost to shreds and kept only for sentimental value or to be cut up and reused, and fresh new ones, made ready to replace the ones that were falling apart.

There was also, at the bottom of the chest and carefully wrapped in crackling yellowed paper, her parents' wedding quilt, stitched by her mother and the women from her family. This one was never used; it had graced the bed on her parents' wedding night, but since then its yellow-gold and cream ring pattern and exquisitely delicate quilting had rarely seen the light of day. Aillean thought it was beautiful, but she had understood from the earliest age that this quilt was never to be got out and used as an impromptu tablecloth, or taken out into the garden to act as a picnic rug, or subjected to any of the indignities that the more workaday quilts occasionally had to suffer. This one was special.

Now she pushed and shuffled her blocks around in front of her, trying to make a pleasing pattern with them. She was working with a simple four-square design, each block made up of four identically sized squares of fabric stitched together, first in pairs and then two pairs joined to make a square block. These blocks would eventually be joined in rows and then the rows stitched together to form a small quilt for her own bed.

For fabric she had been given the pick of her mother's oddments box, which contained all the precious scraps that had found their way into the family's life. Most had been salvaged from clothes or older quilts, but some had been given or traded by other women, and some had even been bought specially for a particular project – like the wedding quilt. Those pieces were especially precious, hoarded against … well, Aillean didn't know what against, really, except that her mother would sometimes get them out and lovingly fold and refold them before placing them carefully back in the box.

In her scavenging through the collection she had tried to pull out a mixture of dark and light fabrics to use in her quilt. Beyond that, however, she had given no thought to the play of colour in her overall design, simply taking the fabrics that pleased her or reminded her of that dress, or that occasion, or that person. Now, with her blocks all arrayed in front of her, she realised as she arranged and rearranged them that the look of her finished quilt was definitely going to be what her mother would call scrappy. No fabric was used twice – at least, she didn't think so – and there was a headache-inducing mixture of floral fabrics from her mother's and her grandmothers' old dresses, plain homespuns, a couple of plaids, a few silks, and even a piece of lace from a tatted tablecloth that had long since fallen to bits. The hues ranged from white, along pale pinks and greens, through lilac and orange, and onwards into deep jewel tones like the piece of dark red silk damask her mother had bartered from a travelling tinker and the deep forest-green velvet that had come from a worn chair covering that her father had foraged from goodness knew where.

She stroked the fabrics as she moved them around in front of her, and sighed as she tried in vain to make a pleasing pattern out of the blocks. From the other side of the room her younger sister sniffed disapprovingly. Marthe had been given the pick of the same oddments box as Aillean, but rather than choosing at random the pieces that pleased her, she had somehow emerged with her hands full of fabric scraps that toned and matched beautifully. She had gone on to turn her pieces into stylish and colourful quilts, simple in design but carefully thought out and beautifully worked. Aillean's own quilt, she realised, would probably end up looking rather like someone had picked all the flowers and foliage out of the garden, spread them all out on the floor and then sneezed on them.

Her mother moved from the stove to stand at her side. She put her hands on her hips and her head on one side, watching as Aillean shuffled the blocks around and formed random patterns with them. She pursed her lips.

"Perhaps if we put some sashing in between the blocks, to break up the patterns a bit," she murmured half to herself, reaching over Aillean's head to move a block into alignment and frowning slightly as it became clear that it was not exactly the same size as its neighbours. "Or … we could put them on point, like this—" She rotated a few blocks so that they stood on one corner instead of on a flat edge, but then shook her head and returned them to their original orientation. "No, that will make it even fussier. It's certainly going to be … well, it's going to be yours, my love. Be proud of it." She mussed Aillean's hair and returned to the cooking. Marthe smirked again.

Aillean snorted quietly. Pride in her work was not something that occurred to her when she thought of her quilt; rather, she was simply keen to get it finished so she would never have to look at the wretched thing again. When it was done, as far as she was concerned it could be consigned to the bottom of the cedarwood chest for ever, tucked away underneath the wedding quilt and forgotten about.

Except that she knew this was not the only quilt she would be expected to make in her life. Needlework was a women's mystery, a utilitarian domestic skill that nevertheless allowed an expression of creativity and individuality in otherwise drab and dreary working days. Women took pride in their needlework skills, and no bride would think of going to her wedding bed without a dower chest containing at least three quilts she had worked herself – her wedding quilt, an everyday quilt for the bed she would share with her husband, and a small coverlet ready for the first baby.

Aillean gathered up her mismatched and oddly shaped blocks with a small moue of distaste. She piled them up next to her and took up her abandoned needle and thread with a sigh, but just as she was about to make another stab she was saved by the outer door flying open and a blast of icy air rushing into the room, carrying with it the sharp tang of smoke and hot metal.

Her mother spun indignantly, wooden spoon in hand. "You shut that door, Cormac Ó Laoghaire, or we may as well all be sleeping outside tonight, for it'll be colder in here than out there!"

From outside came a throaty chuckle, and the sound of someone banging snow from their boots against the stone step. "Sure, and you'd keep me warm enough wherever we were, Dearbhail wife."

Then he was there, filling the doorway and then the room with his massive presence. He threw the door closed behind him, making the shutters rattle, and strode over to the stove to grip his wife around the waist. She struggled half-heartedly, protesting about the supper burning, but she laughed as she berated him and Aillean knew she didn't mean it.

He released her after planting a few hearty kisses on her lips and whispering something in her ear that made her giggle and slap at him with the wooden spoon. Then he reached over and chucked Marthe under the chin, and rested a hand on Aillean's head as she sat at the table. "All my women," he pronounced proudly. "And what have you all been up to today, while I've been sweating my guts out shoeing Old Man Hurt's team of useless nags?"

Marthe piped up first. "Look what I've done, Da!" She waved her perfect seams under his nose, anxious that he should marvel at her precocious talent for needlework. As always, he did exactly that, nodding in pretended understanding as she pointed out her matching corners and then told him that she only had to make three more blocks before she could start assembling her second quilt of the winter. "And Aillean's still working on her first, Da. Look, see how much I've done!"

"Ah, my lovely, you've got neat fingers, to be sure, but Aillean's is a great slow work of magic and beauty. Isn't that right, cailin?"

Aillean looked up at him as he grinned down at her. "Oh, yes, Da. Magic and beauty. That's what it is, alright." She shoved the pile of finished blocks towards him, and then hauled them back before he could spread them out. She was touched by his loyalty, but even though he was a man, and therefore ignorant of how these things worked, she knew he must be able to see that her quilt would be a poor relation when compared with Marthe's neat and co-ordinated creations.

"Supper now, girls," her mother said. "Clear the table – and Aillean, make sure you gather up all your pins this time.

I had to put ointment on your father yesterday after he sat on one you'd left on your seat."

Cormac chuckled again and winked at Dearbhail. "Aye, it's still terrible painful down there, wife. I'll be needing more of your ointment later on."

She giggled again, and then got on with serving out the family meal while Marthe and Aillean cleared and then set the table.

3

Later, when the supper pots had been cleared, washed and put away, Aillean got her patchwork out again. She let out a heavy breath as she contemplated it, and then glanced up to see her mother watching her as she sat by the stove and worked at her own needlework. The needle flashed and the thread sighed softly as Dearbhail expertly stitched two blocks together; she was making a lap quilt for her husband's chair, for him to throw over his knees during the long winter evenings. The muted blues and browns of the fabrics she had chosen were somehow masculine, even though the pattern was a complicated whorl of half-square triangles and points that resembled a many-petalled flower. The design seemed to spin around a central point; Aillean could not even begin to understand its construction, but her mother had almost finished assembling the piece and it would soon be ready for quilting.

Dearbhail saw Aillean's glance, and half-smiled in return. She nodded towards the scraps of fabric in her daughter's hands.

"T'would be nice if yon piece was finished by the time the Cailleach arrives. She'll choose maybe two or three quilts to work with, and you never know."

Aillean scowled. "Sure, she'll never choose mine over Marthe's, or yours, or anyone else's. Whether it's finished or no, there'd be more chance of … of …" she struggled for words, "…of this table getting up and walking out the door."

Marthe sniggered without raising her eyes from her own work, but Dearbhail held up her hand. "Now, child, don't speak so. I've seen the Cailleach make surprising choices before – she works with what speaks to her, which may not necessarily be the most beautiful or the most expertly made. She has her own reasons for her choices, and she rarely explains them."

Marthe put down her needle. "Mam, why does the Cailleach only come once in the year, and then go away again? If she stayed here, she could work with everyone's quilts."

Dearbhail shook her head. "The Cailleach comes when she will – sometimes early in the spring, just after Oimelc, and sometimes later." She shrugged gently. "Some years she does not come at all. She does not explain, just as she never explains anything. She simply walks into the village, sets up her frame in Cairell Maoilfhinn's barn as usual, and waits for us to go to her. One year she did not arrive until just before Bealtaun – we had given up on her that spring."

Aillean nodded. "I remember. That was the winter you made my bed quilt, and you wanted her to work with it. She didn't, though."

"No." Dearbhail shook her head. "That year she chose only one piece, the wedding quilt for Aengus and Lynet. And within a sixmonth…" She trailed off.

"…Aengus was in the ground, and Lynet was with child by another man," Cormac finished for her from his chair by the fire. "Sure, the Cailleach made an excellent choice that year."

Dearbhail rounded on her husband. "Now, you watch your mouth, Cormac Ó Laoghaire. The Cailleach makes her own choices for her own reasons. Who's to say what might have happened if she hadn't worked with that quilt? They might both have died."

Cormac snorted. "Aengus died when a cartwheel ran over his leg and it turned bad. It wasn't a catching disease."

"Even so." Dearbhail's eyes flashed. "You keep your fat nose out of the Cailleach's business, man of mine. Lynet and Declan got wed, and they and the babby are all healthy and happy, and that might well be the Cailleach's doing. Maybe the lass wasn't supposed to marry Aengus in the first place."

"Well, then, why did the Cailleach work on their quilt? Seems to me she'd have done better to..." Cormac began, but Dearbhail interrupted.

"Seems to you, does it? And since when has women's magic had anything to do with what seems right to a man? You keep your nose in your forge and out of what you don't understand." Her eyes were narrowed, and she jabbed her needle in his direction to emphasise her point. "The Cailleach's magic always works, always, but maybe not in the way folk expect."

Cormac subsided with his hands raised placatingly, but Marthe leaned forward. "Why doesn't she stay here, though, Ma? Why does she go away when she's finished her work?"

Dearbhail relaxed back into her chair, her piecing work forgotten in her hands. "I can't tell you that, child. She comes when she will and she goes when she will, carrying that frame of hers on her back the way."

Marthe persisted. "But where does she go? Does she have a house somewhere else? If we made her a house here, she might stay and work on all our quilts."

Dearbhail laughed, pulling her thread taut and examining her tiny stitches. "But then we'd all have the magic, child, and the Cailleach's quilts wouldn't be special any more. She has her round, and she comes most years, but she and her magic are not to be counted on or explained."

She flicked her eyes back towards Cormac. "Or questioned."

"I want her to work on mine," said Marthe, smoothing her work out across her knees. "I want to ask her for a wish to be quilted into it."

Dearbhail looked up. "The Cailleach will not ask you what you want if she chooses your quilt," she said sharply. "She will give you what you need, and there will always be a price to pay."

Marthe blinked, but Aillean nodded, musing. "For Lynet, she needed Declan and the babby, but Aengus was the price," she said quietly, almost to herself.

"Aye, maybe." Dearbhail looked at Aillean with narrowed eyes. She seemed about to say something else, but she stopped herself and concentrated on her stitching instead.

Cormac leaned forward and patted Marthe on the knee. "Another two se'enights to Oimelc, daughter, and then you can start looking out for the Cailleach. Maybe you can help her carry her frame." He chuckled softly.

4

The next two se'enights passed slowly, the land remaining locked in the grip of winter. Aillean and Marthe were unable to leave the cottage for long, if at all, and they passed the days in helping their mother with household chores, working on their quilts, and bickering until Dearbhail threatened to throw them out into the snow where they could take their chances with the cold and the wolves. Marthe finished her second small quilt, and then spent two days trying to decide which was the best, the one she would offer to the Cailleach when she arrived. Aillean gritted her teeth and tried valiantly not to respond to her sister's endless chirrups about how proud she was, and how the Cailleach was certain to choose her quilt, and how she was sure she knew what the magic would bring her.

After what seemed an interminable time the choice was made, and Dearbhail dug out some batting and a piece of backing fabric so that Marthe could baste and begin quilting the unsuccessful candidate. It took her a few days and some very sore fingers before she got the hang of hand-quilting, during which time Aillean had the small satisfaction of watching her sister struggle and bleed as she herself did every time she picked up a needle. Inevitably, however, the younger girl got the knack of it, and before long she was outlining all the motifs on the fabric and wondering aloud what pattern she should use for the border and to fill in the background sections.

Meanwhile Aillean worked doggedly at her own patchwork, trying to turn it into something attractive but fighting a losing battle against clashing patterns and colours, wandering seams, uneven stitching and tangled thread. She even managed to break a needle by stabbing it through the fabric and hitting the table beneath, earning a rebuke from her mother and a stifled grin from Marthe.

Eventually, however, a couple of days before the fire-celebration of Oimelc she stitched the last block in place. Her mother gave her some strips of plain fabric for a border, and she spent a day attaching them to the riot of colour and pattern that she had created with her blocks.

Finally, when she laid the finished piece out on her bed and stepped back to look at it, she was surprised to feel a grudging pride in her effort. Somehow, she realised, the wildly clashing colours and competing patterns in the fabrics had been lashed together into something that almost worked as a whole. There were chaotic areas that jarred the eye, but they were set off by other sections that were mellow and coherent. The layout was artlessly random, the corners of the squares rarely met as they should, some blocks were substantially bigger or smaller than their neighbours and the whole had a definite slant to it, but Aillean felt a reluctant fondness for it. Her own patchwork quilt. The first, and, if she had any choice in the matter, also the last.

She sighed as she regarded it, aware that it was only half-finished; if she wanted to feel true pride in her achievement she would have to layer it atop soft batting and a piece of backing fabric, and then quilt the three layers together. She knew her mother had a piece of soft flannel set aside for her to use as a back, and an old blanket for batting, but she was not looking forward to the next part of the process. Marthe had struggled with it and given herself sore fingers, and she was good at sewing. Aillean hated to think what kind of bloody state her own clumsy hands would be in after a few sessions pushing the needle through the thick quilt sandwich.

She folded the half-done project and placed it in the box at the foot of her bed, closing the lid with a sigh. If she was lucky her mother would forget about it in the preparations for Oimelc, and she might get away without starting work on the quilting for a while yet.

5

I walk into the early twilight and through it into full dark. The night is silver and sharp, the kind of night where a lone traveller can feel the stars looking back at them. On nights like this I am glad of the weight of the frame on my back, for it presses me down and anchors me to the road.

The cold bites my nose and fingertips and the ice cracks in the ruts beneath my feet; it would be tempting to stop and wait for first light, if there were anywhere sheltered and safe. But Oimelc comes with the dawn, and I must be in my place and set up by then.

The road is familiar, of course; I pass this way most years, stopping in the village and staying a night, two or three, sometimes a se'enight depending on the work. The women know me and look out for me; the few years I have been absent there were questions when I arrived the following year, but in this as in all things, my reasons are my own.

On this night my arrival will not be noted. The women and their men will be shut inside their houses and busy with their preparations for Oimelc – bread and cakes baked with flour drawn from their carefully hoarded stores, honey scented with the blooms of high summer, and the autumn's fruits carefully preserved. Tomorrow they will welcome the Bride and ask for her blessing, eat, drink, light fires and sing to celebrate the first stirrings of light and life after the heavy dark of Jul.

My presence will disrupt their celebrations, of course, even while I allow my sudden appearance at the turn of the season to become part of my mystery. In truth I know I am early for them this year; my last stop was shorter than I expected, the work finished inside two days. Sometimes it goes that way, when the magic flows and my needle flies. Perhaps I should have dragged it out, delayed until the days had lengthened and warmed, just a little; the cold this year feels unseasonal to me, more bitter than it should be, although perhaps that is my old bones talking.

But I did not, so now I am driven to keep moving forward through the glittering dark, to get off the hard-frozen road and into the shelter of the barn where I always set up. They will find me there in the morning, and then my work will begin.

6

That night the village and its outlying farms prepared for Oimelc. The unwed maidens had made their brideogs out of straw and ribbon, and were gathered together in Moire Ó Bragain's house to await the calling of the young men with the first light. In another year or two Aillean would join them, but for now she was content to spend the evening with her family, laying her favourite linen blouse out in the snow overnight to be blessed, and raking the ashes in the hearth smooth in the hope of seeing the Bride's footstep as she passed by. Dearbhail baked bannocks, and Cormac brought in a good supply of firewood and coals ready to kindle the hearthfire in the morning.

Oimelc dawned bright and sunny. A sharp frost had settled over the valley where the village nestled, and trees creaked and groaned as the sap froze in their snow-laden branches. When Cormac came back inside after visiting the backhouse there was silver ice sparkling in his beard, and he blew and stamped as Dearbhail worked to light the hearthfire.

"Get on, woman, a man could freeze. The Hag has been out gathering her firewood this morning – it'll be a long winter."

"Hush now. Go stand by the stove if you're that cold – ah, look, there it goes." Dearbhail rocked back on her heels, a small flame alight in the hearth. They all watched as the fire struggled into life, gathering kindling into itself and consuming it with little pops and crackles.

Dearbhail stoked it with a few more sticks and some of their precious store of coal and then stood, brushing ash from her skirt. "Marthe, fetch me the bannocks for warming, and then set the table. Aillean, bring the milk – sharp, now, girls. It's past time we broke our fast."

Aillean sighed, and then started struggling into her outdoor clothing – heavy leather overboots, pulled onto her feet on top of her soft indoor shoes and stockings, an extra knitted jacket, and then a thick fur-lined oilskin and a sheepskin hat and mittens. She would have to take the mittens off to milk the goats, of course, but she knew from experience that even the short trip out to the animal shed could sometimes be enough to make her fingers tingle and then go numb with the cold.

Grabbing a bowl and opening the door, she sucked in a swift breath as the frigid air rushed past her into the house. The cold made her throat ache, and she blinked against the glaring brightness of sunlight reflected off snow.

"Aillean! Close that door!" her mother called, and she took a step forward into the blinding morning and pulled the door closed behind her.

The trip across the yard was short enough to seem like nothing, but long enough that the cold had time to hit the back of her neck and make her shiver. Her breath plumed in the air and trailed behind her, making her smile as she imagined she was a fire-spouting drake, breathing smoke and fumes into the crisp fresh morning. At least then I'd be bloody warm, she thought, and chuckled softly.

She reached the door of the byre and unbolted it, tugging it open and barrelling into the musky warmth within. The billy goat stamped and shook his head in challenge, dancing skittishly away from the door and then planting himself four-square in the middle of his pen and glaring at her with his slotted yellow eyes. The two nannies, their udders heavy with milk, simply looked up and snorted softly, and the three half-grown kids eyed her anxiously from behind their mothers.

Murmuring softly, Aillean peeled off her mittens and picked up the milking stool that lived by the door, climbing over the partition into the pen with the nannies and their kids. The young ones were initially nervous, as they were every morning, but they relaxed quickly and by the time she had thrown a couple of handfuls of mash onto the ground and settled herself on the stool by the flank of one of the contented nannies, they were butting her playfully in greeting. They were getting big now, and twice she was almost knocked off the stool before they grew tired of their game.

In between butts she milked the nannies as they rooted for the mash on the hay-strewn floor, taking a little from both so there was enough for the family's breakfast but also enough left for the voracious kids. In truth the young ones were almost weaned and ready to be separated from their mothers, but the twice-daily milking would make sure that the nannies' supply continued after the kids had grown. As the bowl filled in soft spurts and gurgles she reflected that here, at least, was something she was good at. Her fingers were nimble and gentle in the milking shed; not for the first time, she wondered why she was unable to transfer the same dexterity and lightness of touch to her sewing.

After a few minutes she had drawn enough milk to break the family's fast. She stood, careful not to tip the bowl, and placed it on a high stone ledge in the wall, out of reach of the animals. Then she spent a short time making sure they had enough feed and water, murmuring her thanks to the nannies as she did so. She did not linger because she knew her mother would be waiting on the milk, but it was bad manners to leave without thanking the creatures for their generosity.

Climbing back out of the pen and collecting the bowl of milk from its shelf, she left the byre, closing and bolting the door behind her. The still-warm milk steamed gently in the frigid air, vapour rising in tiny wafts and spirals and trailing behind her as she walked quickly back across the yard towards the house.

As she neared the door, however, she heard a breathless voice calling her name. Turning and raising a hand to shade her eyes from the blinding glare of the sun on the snow, she made out Neasa Ó Grádaigh, a girl about her age who lived in the village a half-mile distant, swaddled in layers of clothing and struggling towards her along the packed ice that lined the track past the homestead.

Neasa slipped and slid a few more steps, and then halted a few yards from the gate. "Aillean! Aillean, get your mam!" she panted. "The Cailleach is come!"

Aillean's eyes widened. "The Cailleach? This early?"

"Aye," replied Neasa. "She arrived in the night, just blew in through the frost from who knows where. Went straight to Cairell Maoilfhinn's barn, and was there all set up when he went in to feed the beasts this morning."

Aillean blinked in surprise, and then moved to open the door. "Mam!" she called. "Mam, Neasa Ó Grádaigh is come, says the Cailleach is here!"

There was a moment's silence from inside the house, and then a rustle and a flurry as her mother rushed to the door. She stuck her head out into the freezing morning.

"Neasa Ó Grádaigh, are you sure?" she said urgently. "Where did you hear?"

"From Áine Maoilfhinn herself, ma'am. She charged me to run and tell as many folk as I could think of. She said to come when you can."

Dearbhail nodded. "My thanks, Neasa. Will you come in and get warm?"

Neasa shook her head, already turning on her heel. "No, I must be away. Áine is out spreading the word as well. Will we see you later?"

"Aye, that you will, and thank you, Neasa. Go safely." Dearbhail raised her hand in farewell, and stepped smartly back inside as Neasa set off back towards the village. Aillean followed her in and closed the door behind her.

Cormac and Marthe were sitting at the table, each nursing a mug of hot tea. There was a plateful of toasted bannock between them with butter and honey for spreading, and two more empty place settings; clearly the family had been waiting for Aillean's return before starting their breakfast.

Aillean put the milk, already chilled from its journey across the yard, carefully down on the table and glanced at Marthe. The younger girl was open-mouthed and starry-eyed with excitement, her tea forgotten as she gazed at Dearbhail.

"Mam, the Cailleach! Is she really here already?" Marthe's voice went squeaky in her excitement, making her sound far younger than her twelve years. "Can we go?"

Dearbhail was standing in the centre of the room. She clasped her hands in front of her, tipping her head on one side as she considered, and then she gave a sharp nod.

"We will go," she said. "Of course we will go, but we will break our fast first." She moved to the table and sat down, motioning Aillean to do the same. "Eat, girls. Cormac, we'll be gone all morning. You'll have to see to the animals."

Marthe was bouncing with excitement, and was almost unable to eat. She could barely force down a scrap of bannock smeared with honey before she was up and away, getting her best quilt out, folding and refolding it, wrapping it carefully in a piece of spare fabric and stowing it in a backpack for portage to the village. She was ready and waiting by the door, pulling on her sheepskin hat and gloves, while Aillean was still sitting at the table drinking the last dregs of her tea and picking up the final few crumbs of sticky bannock with her finger.

Dearbhail was getting ready too, packing up two patchwork projects that she had made over the winter and putting them carefully in the bag with Marthe's. After a minute or two she noticed that Aillean had not moved.

"Come on, girl, or we'll be going without you," she urged.

Aillean looked up. "Mam, I'm not going. The Cailleach will never choose my poor piece, and I'd rather folk didn't see it. It's mine, and mine it will stay – I'll quilt it myself, if you'll show me how, but I don't want to go with you today."

Dearbhail stopped fussing with the bag and stood quietly, looking at her daughter. For a long moment she gazed at her, and an odd expression crossed her face – a combination of all-encompassing love, sudden clear understanding, and admiration for a hard decision well-made. At the end of that long moment she reached out and took her daughter in her arms.

"Come, girl," she said into Aillean's hair. "Don't bring your quilt if you don't wish to, although I do believe it's better than you think it is. But come with us and meet the Cailleach – it's an important thing. She'll be asking why I brought my younger daughter and not my older, and what will I tell her?"

Aillean shrugged uncomfortably. "Tell her the truth – that my sewing is worse than my singing, and neither should be brought outside the house."

Dearbhail laughed softly. "Again, child, you do yourself down. Your singing is not as bad as you think, and neither is your sewing. I'd like you to come, quilt or no. Will you?"

Aillean sighed and knew she was beaten. "Alright. But I'm not taking my quilt."

"Fair and good," said Dearbhail, planting a light kiss on the side of Aillean's cheek before she released her embrace. "Get yourself ready, then. Cormac, make a flask of tea and pack up a few of those bannocks – we'll eat them later, or give them to the Cailleach. Come now, quickly. We must be going."

7

The walk to the village was cold and bright. Marthe galloped ahead, desperate to get there as fast as possible so she could show off her fine workmanship and find out whether the Cailleach would choose her quilt, but Aillean trudged behind her mother, her head filled with gloomy thoughts about whether she would ever make something she would be proud to bring. On balance, she thought probably not, and she hoped that after this year her mother would not make her visit the Cailleach again.

They arrived at Cairell Maoilfhinn's barn to find the doors half-open and a soft feminine murmur of conversation audible from within. The snow in the yard outside had been trodden flat by the passage of many feet, and when they made their way through the doors the atmosphere inside was warmed by breath and excitement.

The buzz of conversation resolved itself into individual voices as they passed through the doors. There were around twenty women present, all from the village or the surrounding homesteads, along with a smaller number of girls. Looking around, Aillean spotted a number of her friends with their mothers and families; there was Saraid Ó Leannain with her mother and sisters, and Uaine Dubhthaigh with her aunt. She raised a hand in half-hearted greeting, noting as she did so that Saraid looked pleased and proud to be there, while Uaine looked about as excited as she felt herself. Both, however, had fabric bundles clutched in their hands.

Dearbhail was busy smiling, waving and greeting people and looking for somewhere to sit. The barn was large, and while it was not exactly crowded with women, most of the places were already taken. There were groups of women standing, some sitting on hay bales, a few perched on the tail end of a cart that was overwintering in the back of the barn, and one or two sitting or squatting on the floor.

Marthe was dancing with excitement, ducking and peering between people to try and get a glimpse of the Cailleach. Aillean couldn't see anyone she didn't recognise, but she did spot a clear space by the side wall, next to one of her mother's cousins and her daughter. She tugged her mother's arm and they moved over to claim it.

All around them women were greeting each other, chatting softly, laughing, talking and pretending not to pay any attention to the precious parcels they were carrying. By unspoken agreement, however, there was a space kept clear in the centre of the barn, filled by nothing and no one. Bright sunlight spilled in through the half-open door, and the flickering light from shielded oil lamps, their flames carefully covered and their fuel jealously hoarded against the long winter gloom, filled the dark corners of the room. Dust trickled from the rafters and caught in cobwebs, and the air was murky and filled with the sweet earthy smell of the hay bales stacked to the eaves against the far end of the space and the four ewes who were still penned in one corner, their restless eyes darting curiously to and fro.

Aillean leaned against the wall, her hands clasped in front of her as she watched her mother and Marthe join in with the general hubbub. In fact, Marthe was the subject of some attention from the assembled women. She was the youngest in attendance, and Dearbhail was asked more than once, with jerks of the head towards where Marthe was hopping from foot to foot, why she had brought the child. Aillean gleaned a certain amount of guilty amusement from watching as her sister made a small exhibition of herself, but the amusement was soon dispelled when Dearbhail informed people that Marthe had made two passable quilts this winter, and was anxious to show them to the Cailleach. Then, to Aillean's chagrin, the women raised their eyebrows in surprise and approval and directed indulgent smiles in Marthe's direction.

Aillean herself was largely ignored. However, this gave her the opportunity to study the folk around her. She saw competition and pride as well as joy, laughter and hope, but in every face there was a measure of anxiety. News was exchanged, children admired, husbands derided; the women talked and laughed with half their attention, but the other half was focused elsewhere, and for a while Aillean could not make out where.

Then, as she watched from her vantage point by the wall, she gradually became aware that there was a still point in the room, a point around which all the conversation, all the women revolved without ever seeming to. No one looked at this point, but everyone was aware of it, and all the interactions in the room were oriented towards or around it. Aillean looked for it, and found – she was not sure what.

A large rectangular wooden frame, some six feet tall and four feet wide, was leaning against the wall by the door. It had a tall narrow cylinder running down each of the long sides, and an arrangement of screws and bolts to anchor something to them; initially Aillean had assumed it was some piece of farm paraphernalia, but suddenly in a flash of recognition she realised it was a quilting frame. The cylinders were rollers, designed to hold a large quilt securely in place and keep an area of it taut between them, allowing someone – the Cailleach, presumably – to quilt the central area by hand. When that area had been quilted the rollers could be wound on and a fresh area revealed.

There was nothing on the frame at the moment, of course, but everyone was aware of the yawning gap between the frame's upright struts. Every woman and girl in the room – with the exception of Aillean – both hoped and feared that her quilt would be chosen to fill that space.

But where was the Cailleach herself? Aillean looked, but still could not see any unfamiliar faces. She wondered if the Cailleach had gone out for some reason – perhaps to visit the backhouse – and she was about to ask her mother when Áine Maoilfhinn, the wife of Cairell Maoilfhinn and an influential and well-regarded woman in the village, stepped into the clear space in the centre of the barn. She was a tall woman with long blonde hair, greying now, tied in a long braid down her back. She placed a soft bundle of fabric at her feet and then clapped her hands for silence, and the hum of conversation died instantly as if everyone had been waiting for this moment.

"Well, since we're all here, I'll be the first. Welcome, Cailleach – 'tis always a pleasure, the more so because we had not expected you for some weeks yet, what with the weather being so hard. We did not think to see you until the thaw began." There was a murmur of agreement among the women, followed by a short expectant silence.

Then, to Aillean's surprise, what she had taken to be an untidy pile of rags by the side of the quilting frame began to move. It shifted and stretched and became a woman – old beyond imagining, weathered by harsh winters, as bent and twisted as a thorn tree on a gale-wracked moorland. The rags tumbled and rippled and became a cloak, ragged and motley, swathing the ancient woman as she rose to her feet with a surprisingly fluid motion.

Tiny black eyes, set into a face seamed and lined like oak bark and shaded by the overhanging edge of the woman's hood, raked the gathering and settled on Áine standing alone and exposed in the centre of the room. Incredibly, Áine flinched visibly, but then regained her composure and stepped forward.

"Cailleach, you are well come," she repeated, extending her hand.

The Cailleach did not take it; she simply regarded Áine in silence. For the first time in Aillean's memory Áine seemed unsure of what to do. Her hand fell awkwardly to her side, and she smiled nervously, looking around her at the assembled women and then back at the Cailleach. There was another short silence, broken only when Áine cleared her throat and smiled brightly.

"I think…" she said, and then stopped. She looked at the Cailleach, who continued to gaze at her with an unnervingly steady regard. Finally, after a few more moments of uncomfortable silence, Áine dropped to one knee and began to unwrap her bundle.

"I think," she said, her courage returning now that she was no longer locked in eye contact with the old woman, "I'll get this out. I made it before Jul, and it will go to my daughter when it is done. What do you think, Cailleach?"

With that she threw back the plain hessian wrapping and revealed a blush of colour within. She unfolded her work with great care, and women around the room gasped as the complex design was unveiled.

The patchwork consisted of a complicated progression of diamonds and triangles, all worked in shades of red and gold. Colours seemed to spiral out from the centre, forming whorls and whirlpools and creating the illusion of rotation wherever one looked. Aillean caught her breath with the rest, recognising the expert design and workmanship and wondering in a flash where Áine had managed to obtain the quantities and varieties of fabrics in the right shades.

The Cailleach did not move, although a number of women around the room shuffled forward, shoving and pushing gently to get a better view. The old woman simply inclined her head and regarded the piece spread out on the floor before her.

Dearbhail stepped forward. "Áine Maoilfhinn, that is truly a beautiful thing, to be sure, and I feel humble now to present mine and my daughter's efforts." There was a murmur of agreement around the room. The Cailleach's eyes snapped up to look at Dearbhail, but then slipped past her to rest first on Marthe, and then on Aillean.

As the woman's bright black eyes settled on her, Aillean felt goosebumps run up and then down her arms. She felt suddenly awkward and self-conscious, and understood why Áine Maoilfhinn, usually so assured and confident, had faltered. She felt the Cailleach's regard in her bones, was aware that she was being weighed, and although she was not sure what she was being weighed against, she was sure in that moment that she would be found wanting in this as in everything else.

Then Dearbhail was speaking again, although Aillean was not sure what she was saying, and unrolling her own bundle to reveal the piece in greens and whites that she had made as a summer spread for her own bed. The Cailleach's gaze lingered on Aillean a moment longer and then flicked to the patchwork being spread out across a hay bale to a new round of appreciative murmurs from the assembled women.

Dearbhail's action triggered a flurry of activity then, with the winter's work being unwrapped and spread out, hung from carefully-inspected nails on the walls, draped over the cart, held up, and generally laid out for the Cailleach's inspection. Marthe placed her small but perfectly formed effort on the hay bale where she had been sitting, and then stood hopefully behind it, dancing from side to side and occasionally reaching forward to flick away non-existent scraps of hay or straighten out tiny wrinkles and puckers.

Aillean stayed where she was, watching as nervous energy ebbed and flowed across the dusty space. Through all the activity the Cailleach did not move; Aillean could see her black eyes flicking about the room, but she remained motionless until the activity had slowed down and all the quilts were proudly on display. Then, and only then, did she raise her chin and throw back her hood, letting the orange flickering light play on her face.

Her hair was long and the grey of steel pins, pulled back hard into a braided knot at the nape of her neck, but with a clear view of her face, Aillean realised with a start that the woman was not as ancient as she had appeared. Her skin was lined and weathered, to be sure, but no more than Úna Caomhanach's or Ríofach Ó Bragain's, and neither of them were old.

The Cailleach straightened her back and became taller, almost as tall as a man. Aillean wondered at how easily the woman changed her physical aspect, as if she was used to hiding in plain sight and showing her true appearance only when it suited her. With a graceful motion she threw back the tattered cloak from her arms, revealing an astonishing overdress beneath.

The garment seemed to have been sewn from a piece of patchwork constructed out of tiny fragments of other fabrics, some pieces no larger than a fingernail; Aillean caught her breath as she wondered at the work that must have gone into creating it. From her position by the wall she could make out that the overskirt was quilted, but not the detail of the workmanship; it hung heavily from the woman's kirtle and brushed the floor as she began to move.

She took a striding step and stood, looking down at Áine Maoilfhinn's quilt spread on the floor before her. With the same unexpected fluidity of movement she sank to a squat and reached out a hand, laying it on the pieced surface of the fabric. The skin on her hand was a similar weathered brown to that on her face, but the fingers were long and straight, displaying none of the age-gnarled knobs and lumps that came to the truly ancient. Her fingers pinched and stroked expertly, and she flipped the corner of the quilt over to inspect the seamwork on the reverse. Áine's work looked neat and well-finished, but the Cailleach did not comment. After a moment she twitched the corner back over and stood, moving on to the next offering.

Over the next few minutes she worked her way round the room, inspecting each and every quilt that was laid out before her. Never once did she speak; occasionally women would murmur a few words to her, explaining their choice of colour and design or trying to excuse some hidden mistake in their work, but the Cailleach simply looked, touched, and moved on.

After a number of minutes she had worked her way around to where Aillean and her family waited. Dearbhail's green and white quilt was inspected first; Aillean thought she heard the Cailleach sniff, although she could not tell whether this signified approval, disdain or something other. Then she moved on to Marthe's small effort, and Aillean found herself holding her breath, willing her sister not to gabble, or giggle, or otherwise spoil the solemnity of the moment.

However, it seemed Marthe was transfixed with fear, or anxiety, or something else; she did not flinch or make a sound as the Cailleach bent to run her hand over the blues and reds of her quilt, flipped the short edge over to pluck at a seam, and then straightened again.

Aillean let out a small sigh, thankful for their mother's sake that her sister had been able to maintain her self-control – and the Cailleach's regard snapped to her face. Close up the woman's eyes were not black, but a very deep blue, almost purple. Piercing and intense, they bored into Aillean's face and she realised she was holding her breath again.

Aillean held the Cailleach's gaze for a few seconds, but was unable to maintain the contact; almost without conscious volition she dropped her eyes, looking instead at Marthe's quilt, still arrayed on the hay bale at her feet. She blinked and hunched her shoulders uncomfortably, wishing the woman would move on.

"Where is your quilt, girl?" The Cailleach's voice came as a shock, filling the attentive and anxious silence in the barn. It was deep and unexpectedly melodious, her tone beautifully modulated and each word articulated carefully as if speech was an uncommon matter involving conscious thought and effort.

Aillean's head jerked up. The Cailleach was still watching her closely, her head now tipped slightly to one side and a small furrow between her brows. Aillean swallowed, aware of her mother shifting nervously at her side.

"I … it's at home, Cailleach. I didn't bring it."

"Why?"

"Because … ah … because I'm not … it's not good enough. I didn't think…" She trailed off into silence, darting her eyes at the Cailleach's face and then away again.

There was a short silence. The Cailleach's eyes still skewered Aillean to the wall and she felt increasingly uncomfortable. At her side she felt her mother shifting nervously, about to intervene and make excuses on her behalf. Then the Cailleach's chin dipped in an abrupt nod.

"Bring it, girl. I should like to see it." And then she was gone, moving on to the next woman, the next quilt.

Aillean sagged back against the wall, closing her eyes and releasing her pent-up breath in a sharp puff. She turned to her mother, to find Dearbhail gazing after the Cailleach in wonderment. She gave a small shake of her head and looked at her eldest daughter.

"Never," she whispered, so softly that only Aillean heard her. "Never has she asked anyone to bring a quilt before." Her eyes were as wide with shock as Aillean had ever seen them – wider than they had been when Da had surprised her by bringing home a bolt of blue-green silk from the market, wider even than they had been when Marthe had fallen from an apple tree in the orchard and knocked herself out cold for half a bell.

Aillean's heart was pounding. She watched the Cailleach as she moved away from them, pausing to touch and inspect the other quilts on display, and as her gaze moved across the room she became aware that the eyes of almost every other woman in the place were fixed on her. Most were wide with shock, like her mother's, and some were smiling in encouragement, but others – a few – looked hostile, their faces hard and jealous. Aillean blinked and lowered her eyes again.

"What should I do?" she muttered to her mother.

Dearbhail gave a tiny shake of her head. "You must bring the quilt, child. But not now – go later. She is almost done."

Sure enough, the Cailleach was moving back to her original place next to her quilting frame. Eyes gradually shifted away from Aillean to focus on the tall woman, who was now standing by the wall and resting a hand on the smoothed and worn timber of her frame.

There was a small whispered susurration as women shuffled forwards, their faces bright with anticipation, eager hope and a lacing of anxiety and fear. Dust rose from the layer of straw on the floor, settling again as stillness returned. The Cailleach stood, alone and unmoving, her eyes lowered to the floor. Then she spoke, her deep melodious voice ringing out and filling the murky space.

"I can make no choice here."

There was a moment's silence. Women stood stock-still, their minds unable to grasp what the Cailleach had said. Then there was a simultaneous intake of breath, and a recoil as every woman present reacted to the Cailleach's words.

"What? No choice?"

"What does she mean?"

"Why not? Are they not good enough?"

"There are plenty here! Surely Áine's, if no one else's…"

The babble of voices grew in volume as women turned to their friends and relations in horror, and a few folk were even bold enough to take a few steps towards the Cailleach. Aillean glanced at her mother and saw her own shock reflected in Dearbhail's face.

Almost every year for ages past a Cailleach had come, made her choices of the quilts offered to her, and then stitched her magic into them. The women of the village accepted her gift gladly and with honesty. There was always a price to pay, of course, but that was part of the mystery – the few quilts that were chosen became heirlooms, carrying their cantrips down the generations, while their makers accepted their good luck along with the obligation to pay for the Cailleach's investment of time, skill and magic.

Sometimes the price was monetary, sometimes it was in kind with food or other goods, and sometimes it was more intimate and private – in those cases, often the arrangement was kept between the Cailleach and the woman concerned. In rare cases the Cailleach would waive the payment for the time being, but always, at some point, reparation would be required. Everyone understood that the magic was deeply personal and would bring some change in fortune for the makers of the quilts concerned, but it was also accepted that the change would not necessarily be what the maker might expect or want. Always, though, it would in some way be what the woman or her family needed.

Every year the Cailleach had made her choice, until this year, this spring. She had never rejected the entire offering of quilts before, at least not in living memory, and Dearbhail was not the only woman apparently struck dumb with shock. Aillean could hear Marthe bemoaning her luck that her first quilt should be offered in the year that the Cailleach refused to choose, and all around her women were wringing their hands, turning to their friends and relatives in disappointment, surprise and indignation.

Gradually, however, a hush spread outwards from the Cailleach. She had raised her head and was regarding the group, her indigo eyes unreadable. Her gaze travelled slowly from one woman to another, from one family group to the next, and silence followed it as stillness follows a storm. Eventually all were quiet, waiting for the Cailleach to speak.

"I did not say I will not make a choice. I said I cannot make one here and now. I have not seen all the quilts that have been made this winter."

Aillean's stomach lurched, and suddenly she was very glad of the wall behind her holding her upright. The Cailleach did not look at her, but many others did, and a rush of whispers ran around the room. "It's Aillean Ó Laoghaire. She wants to see Aillean's quilt before she'll choose. Aillean Ó Laoghaire!"

Aillean dropped her head, and then glanced up to catch Marthe scowling at her with a mixture of fury and awe, but when she looked at her mother she was surprised to catch an expression of something like pride on her face. Fierce love shone out of Dearbhail's eyes, and she reached out a hand and laid it on Aillean's arm.

"You worked harder for that quilt than anyone I've ever seen," she said in a whisper. "Go, now. Fetch it, and be proud that the Cailleach believes you are worth waiting for." Dearbhail gave her daughter's arm a squeeze, and then tugged her gently away from the wall, dropped a kiss on her hair and gave her a gentle shove towards the door. "Go. You know the way."

Aillean took a faltering step, propelled by her mother's push, and then another. She was only a little surprised when the women in her path to the door cleared the way for her, shuffling to one side or the other to make room. Quilts were picked up and folded protectively over arms, and more than a few people touched her fondly on the back or arms in encouragement as she stumbled past them. Others scowled, however, and one or two turned away. She did not look at the Cailleach as she pushed open the wide barn door and stumbled out into the blinding sunlight.

8

The journey back to the farm passed in a blur. Aillean walked, ran, skidded, fell once, and arrived home in a flurry of ice crystals and pluming breath. She burst in through the door of the house, the warm air inside making her frozen cheeks tingle, and was half-relieved, half-disappointed to find her father absent. He would be at work in the forge, and she briefly considered running across the yard to find him. He would be interested, she knew, but she also realised that he wouldn't really understand the importance of what had happened; she wasn't sure she understood herself, in truth, and she found she could not take the time to explain.

Instead she clattered through to the bedroom she shared with Marthe and retrieved her quilt from the wooden chest at the foot of her bed. It was wrapped in a clean piece of sacking to keep it safe and she could simply have lifted it out of the box and set off back straight away, but she could not resist unwrapping it to inspect it privately one final time before it was exposed to the Cailleach's scrutiny.

As she unfolded it on her bed she was struck anew by the clashing mixture of colours and patterns. Plaids and checks competed with florals, homespuns and plains, with every colour of the rainbow represented at some point in the design. Design. She chuckled to herself as she reflected that there had been very little conscious design in the construction of this piece of patchwork; fabric squares had been selected more or less at random, and sewn together without regard for harmony or balance.

And yet, somehow, unexpectedly, the final piece worked. Perhaps it was the plain cream-coloured borders that drew the disparate parts into a whole, or perhaps it was simply an accident of the random placement of the squares, but as she regarded it Aillean found herself drawn into the pattern. She could see how certain colours were placed boldly in some areas and echoed more softly in others, how juxtapositions occurred and recurred throughout the design, and how the whole had an unexpected symmetry and clarity. She could see that the quilt was not traditional, except insofar as it was made from recycled scraps, but she realised for the first time that it might, to some eyes, be beautiful.

Shaking her head, she folded and re-wrapped the bundle, tying the sacking closed with a piece of cord and tucking it under her coat. She took a moment to check the banking of the hearthfire and the stove before sliding out again into the snowy morning, closing the door carefully behind her and starting the trek back to the village, Áine Maoilfhinn's barn, her mother, and the Cailleach.

Arriving a quarter bell later, Aillean paused for a moment outside the barn. She took a few seconds to compose herself, slowing her breathing and smoothing down her hair, some of which had escaped from its braid during her energetic walk. Then, drawing a deep breath, she pushed open the door and walked steadily inside.

The warm air stroked her face as she closed the door behind her, the gentle caress making her frost-chilled skin tingle. Concentrating on latching the door to stop it swinging open again, she became aware that the hum of conversation which had been audible from outside had ceased, and as she turned to face the assembled women she was the only person moving in the room.

Her eyes sought her mother first, and she took a few steps towards her, extracting the sacking parcel from under her coat as she moved. Her mother moved too, however, raising her hand to stop Aillean in her tracks and shaking her head fractionally. She gestured with her eyes towards an area of the room where Aillean had studiously avoided looking – the section of wall containing the tall wooden quilting frame, and next to it the Cailleach.

Reluctantly, slowly, Aillean turned to face the tall grey-haired woman, keeping her eyes focused on the ground. Someone had found the Cailleach a stool, and she found herself looking at the woman's feet and knees drawn up before her.

She took a hesitant step forward, and then another, holding the fabric bundle containing her quilt out in front of her like a ceremonial offering. She came to a point about four feet in front of the Cailleach and found she could go no further; instead she sank to her knees.

"I brought…" she began, but her voice emerged as a strangled squeak. She cleared her throat and tried again.

"I brought you my quilt," she managed, still holding the bundle in front of her. She proffered it forward, but after a few moments when the Cailleach made no move to take it she risked a glance up at the woman's face.

She was surprised to see the Cailleach was smiling gently, almost fondly at her. She made a small gesture with her hands.

"Spread it out, then, girl," she said in her melodious voice.

"Oh – ah, yes, of course." Aillean fumbled at the cord holding the bundle closed, picking at it with fingers made clumsy by embarrassment and cold. After what seemed like an eternity the tie fell away and she placed the bundle on the floor, pulled the sacking aside and unrolled her quilt.

As she spread it out in front of her the Cailleach shifted, leaning forward. All around the room the other women were also moving, shuffling and pushing in a slow dance as they all tried to see the quilt the Cailleach had specifically requested. Aillean twitched the fabric straight on the floor and then sat back on her heels; she kept her eyes on her hands, now folded in her lap, and waited for a reaction.

For a short while there was no sound apart from the murmurs of women in the back rows as they complained they could not see. The Cailleach was silent and still, and the women who had clustered around as Aillean unrolled the quilt were also quiet, peering at it as it lay on the ground before them. Aillean concentrated hard on her hands, twisting her fingers together and willing herself to remain calm.

After a time that might have lasted minutes or no more than a few heartbeats, the Cailleach reached down and placed her hand on the fabric of Aillean's quilt. She stroked it gently, and then flipped the corner over, exposing some of the uneven seam allowances and ragged stitching. She ran her fingers slowly along one of the seams, and then folded the corner back over, straightening out the quilt and tugging it gently into place. Then she sat back on her stool.

"Thank you, girl," she said simply.

The spell holding the other women was broken, suddenly and completely. Hands started reaching over Aillean to touch, stroke and examine her quilt; she was jostled from behind, and almost fell forward onto the fabric in front of her. Murmured comments reached her ears from all directions.

"What's so special, then?"

"Look how far out the points are here!"

"The colours! Oh, my dear!"

"I rather like it – not bad for a first attempt."

Many of the voices were encouraging, but some were not; the quilt's, and therefore Aillean's, shortcomings were pointed out, and a couple of women even laughed aloud. Above all there was a palpable sense of relief – this quilt was not the finest in the room, or the most expertly worked, or the best designed. In fact, there was little to recommend it; many wondered aloud why the Cailleach had insisted on seeing it at all.

Amid the cacophony of voices a hand landed gently on Aillean's shoulder. Twisting, Aillean saw that it belonged to her mother, who wore a small forced smile. "Bring it over there, child," she said, indicating the quilt with a jerk of her chin and then nodding towards where Marthe still stood against the wall.

Understanding, Aillean turned and quickly refolded the quilt, bundling it up with its sackcloth covering and scrambling to her feet as the forest of hands withdrew. The Cailleach still sat unmoving as she pushed her way through the crowd of women back to her place with her mother and sister, depositing the bundle of fabric unceremoniously on the hay bale next to Marthe's carefully displayed offering. Her younger sister favoured her with a glare, but her mother dropped a light kiss on her forehead.

"Well done, girl," she whispered. Aillean grinned weakly in response.

Turning, she resumed her original position against the wall. The women that had spilled into the central area to see Aillean's quilt were also returning to their places, carefully stepping over and around the other quilts that were still spread around the space. The Cailleach remained motionless on her stool.

Only when everyone was still and quiet did the Cailleach move. Unfolding herself from her low seat with the same surprising grace and fluidity she had shown before, she stood and took two short paces forward, so that she stood over Áine Maoilfhinn's astonishing red and gold quilt where it lay on the ground. Someone had kicked up a corner of it in the rush to see Aillean's quilt, and the Cailleach leaned down and twitched the fabric so it lay flat again. Then she straightened and allowed her gaze to travel around the room.

This time she did not make eye contact with anyone; her eyes rested solely on the quilts, travelling from one to the next as they were displayed by their owners. People sensed that a choice was about to be made; hands reached out to straighten or rearrange, edges were wafted or shaken to catch the flickering lantern light, and minute specks of dust or wisps of hay were picked off. The air of expectation, shattered by the Cailleach's unprecedented request for Aillean's quilt and the ensuing hiatus while she fetched it, abruptly reappeared.

The Cailleach finished her visual circuit of the room, turning slowly on the spot as she laid eyes on every quilt present. Then she took a step back so that she was standing in front of her quilting frame, facing the women gathered in the room. She took a breath.

"My choice is made," she said, and there was a soft exhalation from the gathering – a sound of relief, excitement, nervous anticipation. Women leaned forward in their eagerness; eyes were wide with anxiety, and some women linked hands or slipped arms around each other's waists. One or two closed their eyes.

The Cailleach raised her chin. "I will work with Áine Maoilfhinn's quilt, and Aillean Ó Laoghaire's. The rest you may work on yourselves. Thank you."

Abruptly, as if that speech had exhausted her verbal resources, the Cailleach turned away from the group and busied herself with adjustments to the quilting frame leaning behind her. She either pretended or really did not notice the ensuing moment of silence, followed by a sudden outburst of whispered outrage.

"Áine Maoilfhinn's, yes, it's the finest here, but the Ó Laoghaire girl's?"

"What could she possibly see in that one?"

"Mine is better than hers!"

"She didn't even bring it in the first place!"

"I'd be ashamed if it were me."

Some women came to Aillean, touching her shoulder or her arm and seeming genuine in their congratulations, but many looked askance, glancing sidelong and whispering to their friends and relations. Aillean felt the buzz of outrage and jealousy wash over her, and she took an unconscious step back, pressing herself even tighter against the wall.

When the Cailleach's pronouncement had come, Aillean had almost fallen. Her knees had buckled, and only Dearbhail's hand shoved hard under her arm had saved her from folding to the floor. She blinked, still unable to believe what she had heard.

"Did she mean yours?" she hissed to her mother, and Dearbhail shook her head fractionally.

"No, child. Yours," she breathed in return. "Chin up, now. Be proud."

But proud was the last thing Aillean felt. A slew of emotions flooded her as women started to leave the barn, their bundled quilts under their arms or their coats. She didn't know what she felt; confused, astonished, amazed – yes, all of these, but also angry, at the women for their reaction and at the Cailleach for seemingly engineering the whole situation, and deeply miserable. She did not feel she had earned any right to the Cailleach's work – in fact, entirely the opposite. Her stitching was so poor that the Cailleach's legendary and magical quilting would clearly be wasted on a piece that would probably fall apart the first time it was washed. Marthe, who had made much more progress towards mastering the skills of needlework, surely had a greater right to the dubious honour; in fact, almost anyone in the room had more right. Her mother certainly did.

And then there was the question of what the Cailleach would ask in return. For there was always a price; everyone knew that. It was private and personal between the Cailleach and the woman whose quilt she was working on, but Aillean had the sinking feeling that it might be something she did not wish to offer or give up. She knew she would have no choice, though – that was just the way things worked.

Women continued to file out of the barn in ones, twos and small family groups. Some looked pleased for her, and a few smiled even though their eyes told a different story, but one or two looked actively hostile, and one woman – Gráinne Ó Floinn, a farmer's wife from the other side of the village, made a furtive warding sign as she passed. Dearbhail stepped after her.

"Now, Gráinne Ó Floinn, you take that back," she said, loudly enough for others to hear. "My daughter has as much right as your own girl to be here, and the Cailleach's choices are naught but her own. You should know that."

Gráinne had the grace to look abashed, and glancing at Aillean she made a conciliatory gesture. Aillean caught her eye and held it for a moment, but then she glanced away, unable to maintain eye contact. Gráinne smiled grimly and moved on, out of the door and away into the freezing sunlight outside.

After a few minutes the only women left in the barn were Aillean, Dearbhail, Áine Maoilfhinn and the Cailleach. Even Marthe had left, drawn outside by a couple of her friends who were anxious to know what enchantment Aillean had worked on the Cailleach. She had gone with a couple of backward glances at Aillean, still leaning against the wall, her eyes shocked and resentful but with also a hint of grudging respect.

Aillean herself did not move. Her shock at the Cailleach's words had not subsided, and she found she was afraid to step away from the support of the barn wall in case her legs betrayed her and she crumpled to the floor. Her breath came fast and light, and her head felt unsteady on her shoulders. Dearbhail's hand rested on her arm, but she felt as if she was somehow distant from the scene, looking in on it from above and to the side.

She watched as the Cailleach spoke a few words with Áine Maoilfhinn, the two women nodding and smiling together like old friends. As they spoke Áine packed up her quilt, folding it carefully into a neat rectangle and then wrapping it in a length of white sheeting. She placed it reverently on the ground near the quilting frame.

Their voices were too low for Aillean to hear what they said, but it was clear that Áine was pleased with the outcome of the conversation. She ducked her head in thanks, and then took the Cailleach's hand in both of hers, holding it tightly and pressing it with her fingers. The Cailleach smiled gently and placed her other hand on top of Áine's as they clasped together, and then the two women parted. Áine walked carefully but swiftly out of the barn, pulling the door closed behind her and leaving Aillean and her mother alone with the Cailleach.

Dearbhail stirred, whispering in Aillean's ear. "Áine's girl Caoimhe is to be wed come spring. A quilt from the Cailleach will be a fine bride gift."

Her mother's words filtered through to Aillean, and she stirred from her shock-induced stupor. Pushing herself away from the wall, she staggered a step and then drew herself straight and upright as the Cailleach turned from Áine's quilt bundle to face her.

Aillean raised her chin to meet the older woman's gaze, and was surprised to discover that the indigo eyes, which had been so terrifying in their piercing intensity, were now crinkled in a gentle smile. The Cailleach took a step towards Aillean and held out her hand.

"I am sorry if you were … alarmed. The ceremony of the moment is important, but it can be too much."

Dearbhail moved to stand behind her daughter. "It was not well done, Cailleach."

The Cailleach shook her head. "I know, but it needed to be done right. There must be no question with this one."

The Cailleach's hand was still outstretched towards Aillean, but she turned it over and made it into a beckoning gesture. "Come, girl. Bring me your quilt, that you were so anxious I should not see."

Aillean blinked, and then bent to retrieve the quilt from where it lay, bundled up on the hay bale at her side. It unfolded itself as she moved it, cascading and rippling with sudden grace over the side of the bale to puddle on the floor. Her face reddening, Aillean gathered it up and walked forward into the centre of the room with it in her arms.

The Cailleach gestured. "Lay it out flat, girl. I believe you do not see it for what it might be."

Dearbhail helped Aillean spread the quilt over the cleared and swept floor, twitching it straight and flicking away stray bits of hay and dust. The Cailleach watched, her mouth curved in a small smile. When the quilt was laid flat Dearbhail and Aillean stepped back and the Cailleach made a slow circuit, stopping a number of times to crouch down and examine details of piecing or fabric placement. Aillean cringed with embarrassment as areas of uneven stitching or mismatched piecing were touched or stroked, and she had to force herself to stand still and not rush from the room, the Cailleach, her quilt.

When the woman had finished her perambulation she stopped between Dearbhail and Aillean and sighed, a small sound almost of resignation. Aillean winced again.

Dearbhail glanced sidelong at the Cailleach. "What is your bargain?"

Still regarding the quilt, the Cailleach tipped her head on one side, an oddly birdlike gesture. "For this one? Nothing."

Dearbhail's gaze sharpened. "Nothing? Come, Cailleach, there is always a bargain, always a price to be paid. If it is something my girl cannot give you, I will pay it."

Aillean turned her head so that she could see both the Cailleach and her mother. Unexpected courage, tempered by the remnants of her anger, welled up inside her like the first bubbling of springwater after a drought.

"No, Mam. I do know that if there is a price, I must pay it myself. And I also know that there is always a price. What would you have of me, Cailleach?"

The Cailleach took a breath, held it for a second, and then sighed it out with a rattle and a cough. Her shoulders slumped, and suddenly, unexpectedly, she crumpled as Aillean had almost done earlier. Her legs all but gave way beneath her, and if Dearbhail had not caught her by the arm she would have fallen. Startled, Aillean reached out without thinking and grasped the woman's other arm and helped

Dearbhail guide her to a hay bale where she sat, wheezing and gasping for breath.

"Cailleach, are you well? How may we help you?" Concern was evident in Dearbhail's voice as she knelt before the older woman. "A drink, perhaps? Aillean, fetch the flask of tea from my bag. Quickly, now."

Aillean scurried to fetch the thick leather flask wrapped in soft insulating wadding. The tea inside was still warm even after its journey through the gelid winter air, and it steamed gently as Aillean poured a quantity into a wood-turned beaker and held it out to the Cailleach. The woman accepted it gratefully and sighed as she took a sip.

"I thank you," she said as her breath returned. "I fear I am no longer as young as I was, and I travelled through the night to arrive in time for this morn."

Aillean frowned. "Why? Tomorrow would have done, or a week. No one expected you this early."

The Cailleach looked up, her lips pursed in what might have been a tight smile. Dearbhail frowned at her daughter, but Aillean would not be cowed.

"It's true, Mam. You said so yourself; one year she didn't come till Bealtaun, and she's always after Oimelc."

The Cailleach shook her head. "No, child. Your mother is right, I have sometimes been later, but now, this year, it was important for me to be here on this morn."

"But why?" Aillean persisted, disregarding her mother's frown and gestures to be still. "I don't understand."

The Cailleach looked up, and said sharply, "Of course you do not understand, girl. You are not the Cailleach."

There was a moment of silence then. The Cailleach took another sip of Dearbhail's tea; Aillean stood at her side and scowled at her quilt, still laid out on the floor in front of them.

Abruptly she moved, stepping forward and gathering the quilt up. Carelessly rolling it around her arm she turned to face the Cailleach head on.

"I thank you, Cailleach, but I do not wish you to work on my quilt," she said in a firm voice. "I want no favours; I will take it home and quilt it myself. Please choose someone else's – my mother's, or Marthe's, or anyone's. They are all much better than this one. I did not want my quilt to be here in the first place, and the decision to take it away again must be mine to make."

Half-way through this speech Dearbhail had taken a step forward and tried to speak, but the Cailleach had silenced her with a short chopping hand gesture and allowed Aillean to finish. The brief echoes of her defiance faded into the dusty shadows of the barn, and there was a short silence.

Suddenly, unexpectedly, the Cailleach chuckled. Bending forward to place the wooden cup on the floor at her feet, she straightened slowly and tipped her chin up so that she could see Aillean's face. Her eyes crinkled again in the same gentle laughing expression, and she shook her head.

"Ah, now, I deserved that. But take it away? No, girl, I cannot let you do that. See, that quilt holds both your future and mine in its stitches."

Dearbhail took a sharp breath, but Aillean narrowed her eyes. "What do you mean?" she asked suspiciously.

"I mean, girl, that this is no favour, offered from the goodness of my heart. I am long beyond that – I must work on your quilt, and you must let me. There is more at stake here than you know."

Aillean shook her head. "I must? No. You will not demand it. If it is so important to you, you will ask me, or I will take it away."

Dearbhail gave a small squeak, and placed a restraining hand on Aillean's shoulder. She began to babble an apology, but again the Cailleach raised a hand, an unreadable expression on her face.

"No, Dearbhail, the girl is right. She did not offer this quilt; I ordered it to be brought, and in doing so I brought her to unwelcome attention. And she is also right that the quilt is not perfect. But for my purposes, I could not choose any other." She shifted on the hay bale as if she was in pain, but her indigo eyes as they sought Aillean's green ones were clear and bright.

"Aillean Ó Laoghaire, will you give me leave to work on your quilt? I will stitch magic into it to bring you and your family love, luck and happiness, or whatever else you might wish, and I ask nothing in return except what you might choose to give."

Aillean blinked, and her eyes narrowed. "What do you mean, what I might choose to give?"

"Exactly that, girl. If you choose to give me anything in return for my skill and my time, I shall be grateful. If not, then well and good, and you shall have my work for free. What is your answer?"

Suddenly helpless, Aillean looked at her mother. Dearbhail, her mouth open in a small O of surprise, gave a small shrug, but then jerked her head in a tiny nod. Aillean frowned, and then nodded herself.

"Very well, then, but I still do not understand. There is always a price."

It was the Cailleach's turn to shrug, a tiny movement of her shoulders that caused her astonishing patchwork overdress to ripple and tremble. "Since you insist – my price is your forgiveness for the upset I have caused you. Do I have it?"

Aillean hesitated for another moment, and then stepped forward and dumped her quilt in the woman's lap. "Aye.

You have it, but I still say you would have done better to choose someone else's."

Whirling, she began to gather the family's possessions. Marthe's quilt was bundled up in its sackcloth wrapping and stuffed unceremoniously into Dearbhail's bag. The leather flask was stoppered, insulated and laid on top of the quilt bundle while Dearbhail, suddenly infected by Aillean's urgency, folded her own offering and swathed it in its protective covering. In less than a minute they were ready to leave.

The Cailleach had not moved. She still sat on the hay bale, Aillean's quilt spilling over her knees. Her hands tweaked and played with the fabric, pleating it between her fingers and then smoothing it out again. She looked suddenly old, shrunken and frail, hunched on the hay bale with her knees covered and her fingers plucking at the quilt. Aillean moved to stride past her towards the door, but as she did so the Cailleach lifted her head.

"Girl, I will be here for a se'enight, working on your quilt and Áine Maoilfhinn's. I would be … pleased to see you here, if you should care to come. I should like to talk with you."

Aillean's breath caught in her throat, and she turned to her mother with an expression of something akin to panic. Here it was, she thought; the Cailleach's work was never free, but it seemed that whatever the woman wanted from Aillean, she was not prepared to discuss it in front of Dearbhail. That could not be good.

Dearbhail put her hand on her daughter's shoulder. "Cailleach, you have scared and embarrassed my girl today, and you have said before both of us that you require no payment from her beyond her forgiveness. This she has granted. If she comes to you, there will be no other price extracted from her."

The Cailleach shook her head, suddenly appearing weary beyond words. "No, there will be no further price," she murmured, looking back down at the quilt. "You have my word. I wish only to speak with her."

Dearbhail nodded once, a fierce and protective gesture, and then propelled Aillean forward and out of the barn into the shattering sunlight.

9

My choice is my own, as always, but this time the reasons are forced upon me. This time I need that girl, that quilt, and it is my great good fortune to have found both when I did. Oimelc is the best time for this magic – perhaps the only time, the Hag giving way to the Bride as the land emerges from the grip of winter.

The mother knows, I think – or suspects. As she leaves, sweeping her girl ahead of her, she looks back at me with something in her eye – a suspicion, maybe, or a threat. Hurt my girl, say her eyes, and I will hurt you. I believe her.

I have no wish to harm the girl, and I will not unless I have to. It is her quilt I need, that she has poured hours and tears and blood into. I need the passion, the resentment, the anger that is sewn into every stitch of it, as well as the determination, the perseverance, the obligation and the love. All of those things are in me too, although they are faded and worn like a many-times-washed counterpane.

Her quilt called to me before it arrived, even before I sent her rushing through the snow to fetch it. It called me as soon as she walked in through the door, with her precocious sister and her calm competent mother. It called me as I looked at all the other offerings, neat and perfect with their matching points and their coherent colours. It called me with its chaos, its resentment, its rebellious temper.

And that is why I must have it. Oh, there is more magic in a single block from that quilt than in all of the others together. There is fire, ice, blood, tears, anger, and sheer ironhard obstinacy. There is also order, family, love, rivalry, tradition, comfort and warmth – all of those things I can take, nurture, and bind into myself as my needle passes through the layers of fabric.

Of course, I will put something of myself into the quilt in return, as I do with every piece I work on. That is why they want me, these women – I give of myself, my vital essence, that their heirloom needlework may bring them luck, or love, or security, or a child, or whatever secret desire they whisper to me when I choose their quilts.

In return, from many of them I take a coin or two, a bolt of fabric, or the promise of hospitality whenever I may need it. From some I take a song, or a story. From a very few I take nothing, because they have nothing I need.

From one in a lifetime I take everything, but they may never know it.

10

The journey back to the farm was swift and silent. A sulky Marthe wanted to discuss the Cailleach's decision and what form Aillean's payment would take, but Dearbhail shushed her repeatedly until she eventually subsided into an offended silence. After that, the sounds of their feet crunching on the compacted snow of the path and her own breath in her ears were the only sounds that accompanied Aillean's thoughts as she travelled the way home for the second time that morning.

She knew she would go back to visit the Cailleach. Even amid her irritation at the way in which the woman had singled her out and made her quilt the undeserving focal point of the assembly, despite herself she was beginning to feel the pride of having her work chosen. Twice during the journey home Dearbhail placed a hand on her arm and squeezed, smiling when Aillean turned to look at her; she knew her mother felt keenly the honour of the choice, and even though she knew that her quilt was a long way from being the most worthy, she was starting to feel the first sneaking and reluctant inkling of pleasure.

She also knew, however, that the Cailleach's unlikely choice would make her the subject of conversation in the town for months if not years to come. As they passed between houses in the village, their footsteps loud in the empty street, curtains and blinds twitched, and once they heard the sound of a heated conversation from a house close to the path, voices hastily shushed as they approached.

Determined not to appear ashamed or humiliated in the face of the village, Aillean squared her shoulders and walked firmly, but resolved privately to find a back way to the Maoilfhinns' barn when she came again.

When the small party reached home, their breath pluming around their faces and their skin flushed with the exertion of their brisk walk, the warm air of the kitchen was a welcome balm. Marthe immediately disappeared into their shared bedroom taking her rejected quilt with her. She muttered and complained but she did not challenge Aillean directly, for which her sister was grateful.

Cormac was still out at his forge, and Dearbhail made a show of busying herself making lunch, so that Aillean was left temporarily alone. She did not remove her outdoor clothes immediately; instead, she pulled off her fur-lined mitten for long enough to grab a slab of left-over bannock from the table and then made her way back outside, shucking her still-warm boots on again at the door.

She clumped off the veranda and around the back of the house, running her gloved hand along the rail and knocking off the night's new fall of snow. Years ago, when she was little and Marthe only toddling, her father had hung a swing in an apple tree behind the house. She made for it now, brushing the snow from the surface of the wooden seat and lowering herself gently onto it, wondering if it would still take her weight. It was months, perhaps years since she had last sat on it and it was lower than she remembered – or maybe her legs were longer, she reflected wryly.

She pushed gently against the icy ground and started herself swinging. The childish activity felt soothing, and the gentle movement of the branch over her head dislodged a shower of tiny ice crystals that made the air sparkle. She took a bite from the crust of bannock and reflected on the morning's astonishing events.

She wondered how long her reluctant celebrity would last. Not long, she hoped, but she lived in a small, close-knit community; she supposed she would have to put up with attention from friends and enmity from rejected quilters for some time to come. She sighed, the slow rhythmic creak of the swing a mournful counterpoint to her thoughts.

Her stunned astonishment at the Cailleach's choice had not diminished, although at least she now felt confident that the woman had not somehow made a mistake. At first she had been sure that the Cailleach had spoken her name in error, and had been certain that she would realise and correct her mistake, calling on someone else instead. Now, however, after their conversation in the empty barn, she recognised that the Cailleach had chosen her quilt, and had meant to do so. She had her own reasons; they were reasons Aillean had no way to fathom, to be sure, but reasons they were.

Aillean blew out her cheeks, sending a jet of curling breath into the freezing air. She could make no guess as to why the Cailleach had chosen her quilt, and in truth she was not sure she wanted to know. The choice had clearly not been made on merit, since her poor effort was certainly not the best, or the biggest, or even the least eye-bleedingly colourful quilt in the barn. That being so, the Cailleach's reasons might not reflect well on the quilt or its maker, and Aillean wondered if it might be wise simply to accept her unwarranted good fortune and not thumb her nose at it by examining it too closely.

Almost as astonishing, though, was the Cailleach's request that Aillean should visit her. Still swinging gently back and forth, Aillean shook her head in puzzlement. She had no desire to visit the woman, but she did want to see how the quilting work was carried out; despite herself she was interested.

She also nursed a small, unworthy but insistent feeling of satisfaction that Marthe, with all her gloating and her perfect piecing, had not been chosen. She knew that her younger sister would be stoking up a head of righteous fury, and a tiny devil whispered in her ear that a casual visit or two to the Cailleach would be a fine way to annoy her sister even more.

The ice chill from the swing was starting to creep through the many layers of clothing between the frozen wood and her skin, so she finished the last chew of the bannock and stood, the boughs of the apple tree creaking again as they were relieved of her weight. Another gentle shower of ice crystals glittered in front of her eyes as the tree shrugged, and she shook her head, releasing a second small fall of ice from her hair. Stamping her feet to warm them, she made her way back into the house for lunch and a grilling from her younger sister.

11

Over the next two days Aillean kept as far away as she possibly could from doing any sewing, thinking about sewing, talking about sewing or even looking at sewing. This was not easy in a house filled with her mother's expert needlework, but she did her best, and once or twice she even managed to put her quilt and the Cailleach out of her mind for a few minutes. Once or twice Dearbhail tried to talk to her daughter about what had happened in Áine Maoilfhinn's barn, but Aillean always found something else to do, or somewhere urgent to go, or something different to talk about, and Dearbhail did not insist.

Aillean's moments of peace never lasted, however, and Marthe's injured sighs as she worked on her own quilting were always enough to bring Aillean back to the remembrance of her invitation to visit the woman at work in Áine Maoilfhinn's barn. Eventually, on the morning of the third day she could hold out no longer. After breakfast she sat by the fire for a time, considering, and then abruptly she got up and began dressing against the weather.

Dearbhail glanced up from where she was preparing vegetables for the evening's stock pot. "You're away to see her, then?"

In the middle of pulling on her thick woollen socks, Aillean nodded. "Aye," she replied shortly.

Dearbhail did not press her daughter further. Instead she stopped chopping winter carrots long enough to wrap a pile of fresh oatcakes in a clean cloth and put them in a small backpack, along with a lump of cheese, a corner of butter twisted in waxed paper and a small jar of last autumn's blackberry jam. She took water from the kettle steaming on the range and made tea in her leather flask, wrapping it closely in a cloth before tucking it into the backpack.

"To share with the Cailleach, or for you alone – whichever feels right," she said as she handed the bag to her daughter. She dropped a kiss on Aillean's head. "Go carefully, girl. There's weather coming in."

Sure enough, as she stepped outside Aillean realised that winter had not yet slackened its grip, no matter that the first green shoots of snowbells were poking bravely through the soil wherever the snow cover was thinnest. Grey-purple clouds hung low in the windless sky, and the air held the heavy promise of snow to come.

As she crossed the yard to the gate she heard Cormac's voice in the forge, raised to berate one of the apprentice lads who had come to work at the farm in the autumn. "Get away from there, ye young idiot! If ye hit it like that ye'll ruin it – now look, it'll have to be redone. Gods save me from apprentices and daughters!"

Aillean smiled as she hurried past the door of the forge. Cormac's relationship with his apprentices was turbulent, but all who knew him also knew that despite his bluster he was an excellent and painstaking teacher, who turned out boys that knew their trade from the ground up. That was why places in his forge were in demand, and when the elder of his pair of apprentices had left at the end of summer past after three years, he had taken on two new boys rather than one. He could often be heard regretting his choice of "three such foolish boys as I ever knew", but Aillean – and everyone else – knew he was fond of them and enjoyed his responsibilities as their teacher. Aillean suspected that he might have wished for a son of his own to apprentice into the blacksmith's trade, but it was clear to all that he doted on his brace of daughters, and he never complained about his lack of male offspring.

Then she was out of the gate and striding away from the farm, the backpack containing her mother's gifts bouncing comfortably in the space between her shoulderblades. The hobnails on her boots dug into the ice on the path and propelled her forward, and she soon settled into an easy rhythm despite the treacherous footing.

As she walked the sky lowered and the air softened, no less cold but heavy now with damp – a wet snowfall was on the way. Darkness came swiftly in the brief days of winter, especially when snowclouds blew in from the north, and although the daylight hours were starting to lengthen Aillean knew that she would need to be home before night closed in or else she would catch a talking-to from her mother.

She made good time to the village, and passed through it just as the first heavy snowflakes were beginning to fall. They settled on her sheepskin hat and oilskin cloak, and she arrived at the Maoilfhinns' barn lightly coated in a sprinkling of fat wet clumps of snow.

Once there, she approached the door somewhat hesitantly. It was pulled to, but there was a crack of light spilling from underneath it. Nervously she raised her hand and knocked, the sound of her knuckles striking the wood deadened by her thick sheepskin mittens.

There was a short silence. The snow settling around her flattened all sounds; a dog barking in a yard somewhere in the village sounded like it was miles distant instead of a few hundred yards. Her breath, coming fast from her brisk walk, sounded harsh in her ears, and she strained to hear any noises from within the building.

As the moment stretched she shifted her feet uncomfortably, debating whether to leave. She determined that she would not knock twice; if the woman was within and had not replied to the first knock, then clearly she did not wish to be disturbed. In an uncomfortable agony of indecision Aillean stayed where she was for the space of a few more breaths, and then finally stepped back and away from the door, turning on her heel to set off back home.

As she did so she heard the scraping sounds of an internal bar being lifted and the door being opened at her back. She spun to see the Cailleach standing just inside the threshold of the barn, limned in the soft orange glow from a number of shielded oil lanterns. The light spilled outside through the open doorway, and fluffy wet snowflakes drifted inside to fall on the Cailleach's patchwork overdress.

They eyed each other for a few wary seconds before Aillean stepped forward, shucking her shoulders out of the backpack containing the food packed by her mother. "I brought this," she said awkwardly, aware that this was not the most graceful greeting she could have offered.

The Cailleach did not seem to mind. She smiled suddenly, creases and lines transforming her face from its usual stern mask into something a good deal more friendly, and stepped back into the building. "Come inside, girl," she said. "We're both getting cold."

Aillean moved through the door and the Cailleach closed it against the weather, putting the bar in place to hold it shut and sweeping a drift of straw along the bottom to keep the worst of the draughts at bay. Aillean put her bag down on a hay bale and began to shed layers of outside clothing, shaking the snowflakes from them as she did so. She busied herself with this for a little longer than was necessary, suddenly unwilling to turn and look at the quilting frame in case her sorry excuse for a quilt was stretched out across it.

When she did turn, however, she was at once relieved and disappointed to see Áine Maoilfhinn's red and gold quilt stretched between the rollers. The frame was tilted and propped on its stand so that the work stretched across it was almost horizontal, sagging slightly between the wooden edges of the frame to allow the Cailleach to rock her needle between stitches and catch all the layers of fabric with her thread. There was a low-backed wooden chair drawn up to the frame so that the Cailleach could sit while she worked, and a heavy blue cloth had been spread over a hay bale to form a makeshift table. Here the Cailleach had spread out her notions and makings – thread, needles and a pincushion bristling with silver pins lay on the cloth surface, and more threads, ribbons and scraps of fabric spilled out of a carved wooden box. On the stretched surface of the quilt lay a bobbin and a tiny pair of silver snips, and a needle trailing a deep golden thread rested at the end of an unfinished line of stitching. Clearly the Cailleach had been hard at work when Aillean had arrived.

Widening her gaze, Aillean noticed a small truckle bed made up in the corner of the barn furthest from the door, piled high with blankets and quilts. The four ewes who had been penned in the far end of the building two days earlier had gone, and their space had been swept clean. A small pot-bellied brazier had been set up there, its metal flue disappearing through an open window padded to prevent draughts, and a scuttle of coal and a basket containing logs and kindling were pushed against the wall. The brazier glowed gently through the grate in its door, a gentle heat expanding from it to take the winter chill from the wide space of the barn.

She caught up the backpack again and turned to the Cailleach, smiling shyly. "My mother – she sent these, for you." She held out the bag.

The Cailleach nodded gravely, reaching forward to take the bag. Opening it she glanced inside, her smile returning as she investigated the contents. She chuckled softly.

"Your mother's oatcakes – and, oh, some jam to go with. If I had not already chosen your quilt, I might almost be tempted to do so simply so that she would send more of that."

Aillean blinked, and then grinned despite herself. Her father often boasted about Dearbhail's cooking, claiming that the Dark Lady of the Otherworld herself might stay her hand for a taste of one of his wife's preserves. It seemed that Dearbhail's reputation was not limited to the fond opinions of her own household.

Clearing a space on her cloth-covered hay bale the Cailleach began to remove the provisions from the bag. Aillean noticed that there was already a covered basket resting on the floor by the wall; it seemed that others were also keeping the Cailleach fed as well as warm. Unexpectedly, she found she was glad of this.

Unsure of herself and what was expected of her, Aillean stepped forward towards the quilting frame. She did not reach out to touch, but she looked closely at the work laid out before her. The quilt was the same intricate piece that she remembered from two days earlier, the deep glowing reds and rich golds of the fabrics placed expertly and precisely to create a swirling pattern of diamonds and triangles flowing out from the central point. Of course, Aillean could only see a fraction of the whole piece because the rest of it was rolled around the timber cylinders at the edges of the frame, but her eyes and her memory extrapolated the rest and she caught her breath at the beauty and precision of the piecing.

Then she examined the Cailleach's quilting, and caught her breath anew. The thread the woman had chosen was a deep gold, almost umber. The quilting stitches were tiny and precise, the pattern a complicated weaving of lines and whorls that spread, knotted, crossed and repeated over the swirls of the pieced design. The quilting thread shimmered against the reds and drew all the disparate golds together into a unified whole, coiling and writhing over the points and edges of the design and softening the lines to make the quilt seem to flow and billow under her eyes.

Almost against her will, Aillean found herself leaning in closer to examine the work. She became aware of the Cailleach at her side, also leaning over the quilt, and glanced up at the woman to see a small smile curving her lips.

"What do you think?" the Cailleach asked softly.

Aillean did not speak. She shook her head fractionally, her hand reaching almost without her volition to touch the intricately quilted section of the work, but the Cailleach's sudden breath made her snatch it back.

"Please, do not touch the quilt, girl. The magic is..." The woman paused. "It is complicated to explain, but the magic is tied to me, the quilt and its maker. If you were to touch it before the work is complete, there might be ... unexpected consequences." She shrugged slightly. "I have seen it happen."

Aillean drew back and glanced sidelong at the Cailleach. "What do you mean?"

The woman hesitated, and then puckered her mouth slightly in a small moue of distaste. "If the person who touches the quilt means ill towards the maker, or towards me, that ill feeling can be captured in the work. The magic may be contaminated, and can have unexpected or unpleasant effects. It is unpredictable at the best of times; it is only my skill with the needle that tames it and binds it into the stitching."

Aillean glanced at her sidelong. "I do not mean Áine Maoilfhinn ill. Or you."

The Cailleach cocked her head. "You did the other day, I think." But then she smiled. "I did not mean to suggest that, though. Just that it is always safer to keep the magic as clean as I can."

Aillean nodded; she barely understood, but she did not question further. Instead she looked around at the inside of the barn, a space made unexpectedly warm and comfortable by the small trappings brought by the Cailleach herself or provided by the village.

"Have you … is my quilt done?" she ventured after a moment.

The Cailleach shook her head. "No. Yours will take … well, I would prefer the minimum of distractions when I am working on it, and Áine Maoilfhinn calls in at least three times a day to see how I am progressing. Once I have finished the work on her quilt my days should be…" she paused delicately, "…quieter."

Aillean suppressed a smile. Áine had the reputation of a woman who could talk, and then talk, and then talk some more; Dearbhail had once muttered under her breath that if words could wear away stone, the land where the Maoilfhinns' farmhouse stood would be as flat as a flood meadow.

There was a short silence. Aillean stood awkwardly in the Cailleach's temporary living space, unsure what she should do or say. The Cailleach herself seemed momentarily distracted; she bent over the quilting frame and picked up her needle as if she was about to take up her work where she had left off, but then she seemed to remember Aillean's presence and turned – perhaps reluctantly – away from the quilt.

"Well, girl, shall we eat? You have walked a good way, and I have not broken my fast this day. I trust your mother has packed enough for two."

Aillean smiled warily. "Aye, that she has. It certainly felt heavy enough to provision the both of us."

The Cailleach chuckled, a low and musical sound. "Then we must make sure it is lighter for your return journey. Come." She seated herself on a low stool next to her cloth-covered hay bale, and motioned for Aillean to join her.

For the next few minutes they ate in companionable silence. The Cailleach contributed a few pieces of dried apple brought by Neasa Ó Grádaigh's mother, and Aillean was surprised by how hungry she was. After all, it was not long since she had broken her fast, but it seemed that her walk through the cold and the snow had stimulated her appetite.

Despite her claim that she had not eaten all day the Cailleach partook only sparingly, although she tasted everything that was provided. When they had finished Aillean rewrapped the remaining oatcakes and placed them carefully to one side for the Cailleach to have later, along with the jam and what was left of the cheese. The flask of tea, still half full, she sealed and placed back in her bag. Then she sat, still and quiet, simply watching the older woman.

After a moment the Cailleach raised her astonishing indigo eyes, caught Aillean watching her, and half-smiled. She lifted a shoulder in what looked almost like a defensive gesture, and clasped her hands together in her lap as she sat on her stool.

"You'll be wanting to know what I meant, when I said I had a matter I wished to discuss with you," she said softly.

Aillean frowned. "Aye, Cailleach, but—" she began, but stopped abruptly when the Cailleach raised her hand in a peremptory gesture.

"Please, girl. I am weary of my title – you, of all people, should know my given name. My mother named me Ríona."

Aillean blinked. She had never, in all the tales she had ever heard about the Cailleach and the enchantments she wrought with her needlework, heard of anyone being gifted with the woman's name. She was more taken aback than she could say, and for a few seconds she simply sat open-mouthed.

After that shocked moment, during which the Cailleach – Ríona – watched her with an amused expression, Aillean collected herself. She bowed her head and stared at her hands, but then, suddenly daring, she lifted her chin and stared the woman straight in the eyes.

"You said me, of all people," she asked boldly. "Why?"

Ríona smiled thinly. "Because of your quilt, girl."

Aillean shook her head, her eyes narrowing. "That is no answer. Why invite me here? It is known that the Cailleach works alone, and that she chooses the best quilts that are offered to her. My quilt was the worst one offered to you – everyone could see it – and yet you chose it. Not only chose it – you asked for it to be brought. You knew what it would be before I had even returned with it, and then you asked me to come here. And now you tell me your name, and suggest that I, and my quilt, are somehow special." She paused for breath. "What is it you want from me, Cailleach?" She laid stress on the woman's title, reluctant to use her given name.

"Very well." Ríona stood suddenly, her intricate patchwork skirt rippling in front of her. Close up Aillean could see that it was worked from tiny scraps of fabric; this much she already knew, but the detail of the quilting had escaped her before. Now she could see it, the lines of tiny stitches forming a pattern of interlocking shapes that sometimes looked like feathers, sometimes like leaves, and sometimes like nothing Aillean had ever seen before. She caught her breath looking at the detail of the workmanship, but then became aware that the woman was standing looking down at her. She scrambled to her feet.

"What I want from you, girl, I already have," Ríona said in a low voice. "I already have your quilt. You may be correct that it was not the most technically accurate piece of work offered to me two days ago, but believe me, I could not have chosen any other."

"But why? I don't understand."

"No, child. You do not." Suddenly she turned on her heel and paced away across the room, towards the small truckle bed against the wall. A pile of folded blankets lay at the end, and from these she extracted a carefully wrapped fabric parcel. Laying it out on the bed she unwrapped the outer layers, revealing Aillean's quilt within.

Aillean rose and followed, standing next to the Cailleach as she unfolded the stitched fabric and spread the quilt out on the bed. As she had once before, Aillean saw the familiar piece anew. She squinted her eyes and looked at the random placement of pieces and the emergent patterns, the arrangement lacking the precision and order of many of the other quilts she had seen, but somehow still coming together to form an almost-coherent whole. Colours bled into one another across whole sections of the quilt, flowing across disparate squares of fabric to disappear and then re-emerge elsewhere. The plain cream-coloured border contained and mellowed the competing colours, framing the whole and turning it from a random collection of scraps into a completed piece of patchwork.

Leaning forward she recognised scraps that spoke to her, reminding her of the night she had pieced that section, or the harvest picnic where Marthe had worn that dress, or the day her father had brought home that bag of scraps. Here was her grandmother's apron, and there was an old cushion cover; here was a piece of heavy cotton damask from an old tablecloth, there was a scrap salvaged from Marthe's favourite rag doll's dress before the doll herself had fallen entirely to pieces, and in that corner was a piece from one of her father's old overalls, washed so many times that the tough blue fabric had worn as thin and soft as flannel.

In places, if she looked carefully, she could see the tiny blood stains from where her needle had slipped and pricked her, and on one patch there was a rust mark where she had left a needle stuck in the fabric for a couple of weeks instead of removing it and storing it in a needlecase as she should have. She smiled softly. This was her quilt, hers and her family's, their lives set out in scraps of fabric in front of her.

Ríona was watching her closely. A small smile played about the corners of her mouth as she read the play of expressions and emotions dancing across Aillean's face. She was silent for a time, but then she spoke, her voice husky and deep.

"Do you see now, child, one of the reasons why I chose your quilt?"

Aillean turned to her, eyes sparkling. For a moment she could not speak; she simply nodded.

"It's…" She choked briefly. "It's my family, my home. It's my mother and my father, my grandmother, my sister. It's bits from all of them."

The Cailleach inclined her head. "It is more than that, girl. It's you. It's what made you, and what you made." She spread her hands. "It is your history, and your future."

Aillean was taken aback. "My history – yes, it's that, for my family and the winter just gone at least, but my future? I don't understand." She realised that she seemed to be saying those words with annoying regularity, but she quelled her irritation and looked enquiringly at the older woman.

Ríona pursed her lips, seeming to consider her words carefully. She moved back across the room to her makeshift table and seated herself on her stool, motioning Aillean to follow.

When Aillean had found a seat on a hay bale the Cailleach took a breath. She folded her hands carefully in her lap and looked up at Aillean, her eyes as deep and dark as midnight floodwater.

"Girl, I am dying. No, listen to me." She held up a hand as Aillean began to protest. "I am old, far older than I seem and you may think. I have walked the seasons of this earth for longer than I dare to recall. In honesty, I do not truly know how many winters I have seen, only that it is many more than the time allotted in the normal run."

She paused for a moment, and then continued. "When I work on quilts, I put myself into them, and I…" she spread her hands, searching for words, "…I deplete. There must be balance in all things, and for the quilts to be more, I must become less. This is my mystery, which I embraced long ago.

"The small payments which I take from the quilt makers are merely gifts in kind; they offer me food for a while, or a roof over my head for a few nights, or a small amount of money to pay my way onward. These are things which I need, to make my way in this world, but they do not replace the essential parts of me that are lost with every stitch I place. And eventually, after tens of years and hundreds of quilts, I reach a point where I am weakened enough that I feel the Otherworld nipping at my heels."

Aillean shivered. A part of her wanted to protest, to tell the Cailleach that she was well and healthy and not old at all, but another, deeper part of her trembled at the secrets being laid before her. She made a small move as if to reach out and grasp the Cailleach's hand, but stopped herself.

Ríona continued. "This has happened before, many times. I weaken gradually over decades, and for a long time no one but myself notices. I tire more easily, my eyes become weak, my fingers tremble and I work more slowly. The magic becomes harder to weave and control, and I begin to make errors. I ignore it for as long as I can; my appearance does not change, at least not that you would notice, but I…" She paused. "I age, girl. And then, eventually, I cannot hide it any longer, from myself or from anyone else. I begin to fail physically – you saw how I stumbled and became dizzy, at the end of the choosing?"

Aillean nodded. "Aye, but I just thought you were tired from travelling through the night."

Ríona smiled wearily. "Tired. Yes, girl, that is it, precisely. I am more tired that you will ever know, but I will not recover with a few nights of uninterrupted sleep. I need … something else, if I am to continue."

Aillean frowned. "What do you need? Can I … is there something I can do?"

Ríona chuckled. "Careful, girl. Your mother would have a choking fit if she heard you offering to help me. She knows that bargains with a Cailleach are binding, and may involve more or other than what you intend."

Aillean swallowed as sudden fear flooded through her, but the woman raised her hand. "Do not fear. I already have what I need – for the present, at least. You have already provided that."

"How … what do you mean? I have given you nothing apart from my quilt."

"Yes, girl. Your quilt." The Cailleach sat back and folded her hands.

Aillean blinked. "My … my quilt?"

Ríona sat forward, her hands on her knees and her indigo eyes suddenly intense. For an instant tiny flecks of light seemed to flow and swirl across their surface, but then they were gone, leaving Aillean wondering if she had seen them at all.

"Your quilt contains everything that you are. You made it, and it contains within it your family, your memories and your history. During the making of it you wept, laughed, slept, bled – and you lived, girl. Every scrap of fabric in it means something to you, and you chose and placed it for a reason. No matter that it is not a perfect example of matched seams or accurate corners – those things are of no consequence. That quilt is a stitched representation of what you are, your emotions, and what your family is and means to you."

Aillean scowled. "Yes, but – how is that supposed to help you?"

The Cailleach smiled thinly. "Part of my magic is the ability to take from a quilt, in the same way I can put something of myself into it. Girl, I intend to take you from that quilt."

There was a silence then. Aillean dropped her chin and stared at her hands, and became aware that they were trembling. Clasping them together she tried to stop their shaking, but they persisted no matter how hard she wound her fingers around each other. For a short while she simply concentrated on breathing.

After a number of careful breaths she looked up, to see the Cailleach watching her with an unreadable expression on her face. Her skin, although wrinkled and pouched, had a luminous glow in the golden light of the oil lamps, making the inky unblinking darkness of her eyes all the more unnerving. Once again there was that illusion of tiny silver sparks dancing across the shining blue, and once again Aillean blinked and they were gone.

Aillean realised that she was holding her most recent breath, and expelled it with a sound that sounded like a gasp in the close dusty air. She released her hands from their grip on each other and laid them flat on her thighs, composing herself to speak.

"Cailleach – Ríona – I do not pretend to understand you or your magic. I do not even think I wish to. You have said you will work on my quilt, and you have said you will not ask me for more than I might choose to give. Bargains with the Cailleach are binding – I know that as well as my mother – and you may not go back on what you have said. But—" She paused, formulating her words carefully. "How can you take me, from my quilt? I am not my quilt."

Ríona smiled, showing her teeth. "No, girl. But you are in your quilt. As you were making it, you soaked into it and through it as surely as if it was part of you. Your emotions – joy, disappointment, love, resentment, happiness, jealousy and all the other things you felt as you laboured over each stitch – all are bound up in it. I can feel them, and I can use them – you will replenish me, and I shall be stronger when I leave here than when I arrived. I shall not be tired anymore."

As she made this speech the Cailleach did not move, but somehow she seemed to lean closer, looming towards Aillean as if she were hungry to drink the emotions and feelings directly from her body. Aillean flinched backwards, but then she straightened her back and summoned a glare.

"That may be so, but you will not have me, and you will not be me. I do not give you leave to take more from me than what you say is in my quilt. That was not our bargain."

Ríona loomed for a moment longer, but then seemed to subside. She sighed. "No, girl. That was not our bargain."

Aillean did not relax. She leaned forward herself, directing her glare straight into the Cailleach's face. "Why my quilt? Why not Marthe's, or my mother's, or anyone else's? They laboured over their quilts just as I did. Why did you send me home to fetch mine when you could have chosen any other?"

The Cailleach frowned. "Not everyone puts themselves into their quilts as you did. Some quilts, the complicated and beautiful ones that cause their makers sleepless hours and involve many decisions – like Áine's, over there on the frame – they do contain something of their maker, because of the emotion and the investment that the woman has made. Others, though, are sterile and blank – the makers did not live while they were making them, they simply sewed the pattern and moved on. Those quilts I can put magic into, but there is precious little there to take out."

Aillean frowned as she nodded slowly, trying to understand. "When I arrived I had nothing with me. How did you know that I had even made a quilt?"

Unexpectedly the woman chuckled. "No magic there – or not much. Your fingers, girl. They are calloused and pricked."

Aillean looked at her hands with some chagrin. It was true – although most of the needle scratches and pricks had now healed after a few days' reprieve from sewing, she still had a small reddened callous on the middle finger of her right hand from pushing the needle through the fabric. She breathed a short laugh.

"True and fair. But how did you know I had … put myself into my quilt? How could you know it wasn't bland and empty, like some of the others?"

"I did not know it for sure, but I saw your sister's and your mother's quilts, I believed you had made one too, and that fact that you had not thought it worthy to bring with you suggested that it might be very different to theirs." She shrugged suddenly. "I took a risk. I knew that I was drawing attention to you, that you would likely resent or even hate me for it, but I needed to see your quilt. And here you are."

Aillean tilted her head on one side. "Here I am indeed." She pursed her lips, considering her next words. "What did you mean when you said the quilt contained my future as well as yours? My past – I see that, although I do not understand your magic, how you can take me from it. But my future?"

Ríona smiled complacently. "Girl, in return for your self that I will take from the quilt, I can put back what you wish me to. I can give you long life, passionate love, many children or none – anything you desire. I can bring you wealth, luck, happiness, fulfilment – the magic in your quilt will outshine that in any others. It will be powerful enough to last your lifetime and on into your children's, and their children's. If you wish it, I can make you an heirloom, and the engine for your family's fortune. Tell me, and I will do it."

12

The girl looks at me with startled eyes. I believe that until that point she had not even considered that her quilt, and my magic within it, might benefit her or her family. She takes a breath, and then another, her face open and transparent as the glittering possibilities flash before her.

She sees her family wealthy and warm, herself in the arms of a rich and handsome man, surrounded by perfect children. She sees piles of coin, a healthy and happy old age, maybe even fame and reputation. She is momentarily inundated by the many and unexpected directions her life might take, all suddenly possible because I can make them so.

Then she surprises me. She turns her face to the expertly pieced quilt on the frame, its colours shimmering and glowing in the dim light. She looks at it with hooded eyes, and then looks back at her own effort, spread on the lumpy bed which is my lot while I stay here. She tilts her head to one side and considers before turning to face me, her eyes alight.

13

"I want to be able to sew."

The Cailleach blinked. "To sew?"

"Yes. My mother can sew, my sister can sew, every bloody woman in the world can sew, apart from me. My fingers don't seem to work that way, but…" She paused, frowning. "But I want them to. I want my mother to be proud of my work, the way she is proud of Marthe's. I want to be proud of my own work. I want you to put magic in my quilt to … to teach me to sew."

Ríona frowned, and sketched a tiny shake of her head. "Girl – my magic does not work like that. It works in generalities, in wide concerns. It can make you healthy, or long-lived, or fertile, but it cannot teach you a specific skill. That is … a different sort of magic, which is beyond my talents."

Aillean narrowed her eyes. "Then can it make me dextrous, or nimble-fingered, or any of the other things I am not, which might help me to be better at sewing?"

The Cailleach tilted her head, seeming to consider. "It can make you ... lucky. And it can help persistence to pay off, so that you will become better with practice. More than that I cannot promise, but I will do it, if that is what you truly desire."

Aillean took a step back and her legs knocked against the cloth-covered hay bale which formed the Cailleach's table. "Then do that, and I will work harder. I will make quilts to make my mother proud of me."

The Cailleach spread her hands. “I believe your mother is already proud of you, girl – prouder than she has said, perhaps. And your quilt – it is not the laughing stock you believe it to be. You have an intuitive eye for design and colour; see how you have placed the scraps in your work, how the patterns echo around the quilt. It is not ... conventional, perhaps, but it is a striking and individual piece. You do it an injustice when you write it off.”

Aillean looked sceptical, and was starting to feel distressed. A sob caught in her throat. “But you’ve seen the seams on the back – there’s scarcely a one that runs straight. The stitches are uneven, and there are more thread tangles than fabric in some places. Sure, the thing will fall apart as soon as it sees any hard use, or the minute it’s thrown in the washtub.”

“You see it with a jaundiced eye, girl. You compare it to your mother’s practiced efforts, and your sister’s precocious offerings. None of them possess the...” Ríona groped for words, “...the life of your quilt.”

Aillean shook her head and spoke fast and low, fighting for control of her voice. “Well then, if you cannot or will not give me that, then I do not want anything. I do not understand the way you say your magic works, and if you wish to weave something of your own choosing into the quilting as a gift, then you have my leave to do so. But I did not ask you to work with my quilt, I did not even want you to see it, and I do not wish for anything from you now.”

She turned and picked up the few remaining items from the hay bale table, stuffing them roughly into the backpack. She was aware that tears were glistening in the corners of her eyes, but for the life of her she could not have said why. The Cailleach watched her with an unreadable expression on her face.

When the bag was packed she began struggling into her outdoor clothing. Coat, hat, mittens and finally boots, all were tugged on while the straight figure of the old woman stood by her makeshift bed, simply watching. Finally, as Aillean fumbled with the lacings on her thick fur boots, the Cailleach spoke.

"Girl, I am sorry if I offended you a second time, or disappointed you. When I am at the full height of my power I am strong, but always my gifts are limited within my own sphere. There are others who could do what you ask; mages from the old Queen's Academy could no doubt give your fingers the dexterity to master sewing and quilting in a day, but I am not of that training, and I am constrained in what the magic will do for me." She shrugged helplessly. "I have rarely been asked for something that I cannot give. Women are usually concerned with safety in childbed, their families' fortunes, or bringing health and happiness to their offspring. All these things I can do. There is only one way I could teach you how to sew, and that would be—"

She stopped short, cutting off in mid-sentence. Aillean looked up to see the Cailleach wearing a peculiar expression, her eyes apparently focused on Aillean's face but at the same time journeying inward, examining some internal landscape. It seemed as though she did not like what she saw there, for her eyes grew wide, and her breaths started coming fast and shallow. Aillean almost moved to see if the older woman was well, but then she remembered how the Cailleach planned to restore her own health. She turned her attention back to her boot, shaking her head.

"It is of no matter. I ... well, I will work harder." She smiled, a hard tight movement of her mouth. "Perhaps next Oimelc when you come, I might have something better to show you. I need to get home now; health and long life to you."

Ríona did not answer, but she seemed to flinch at the traditional words of farewell. She stood aside so that Aillean could stride past, and she did not speak as Aillean kicked away the straw at the bottom of the wide door, exposing a thin line of windblown snow, and lifted the heavy bar that held the door closed. Only when the door had swung open and Aillean was about to slip outside did the Cailleach open her mouth again.

"We will not meet again, you and I, Aillean Ó Laoghaire," she said in an odd voice. "In three days your quilt will be finished, but I will not see you. May it bring you everything it is supposed to."

With that she turned away, and as Aillean pulled the door closed behind her she saw the Cailleach still standing, apparently lost in thought, staring down at her chaotic and unconventional quilt.

14

And so, I think, it ends. In some ways it is a relief – I have always known that my time would not last for ever, but as the days, weeks, months and seasons rolled on I chose not to recall that most of my sisters have already passed from this world.

But this girl? This child, who cannot sew a straight seam, who – when she is offered the world – whose dearest wish is to make her mother proud?

Ah, but was there not a time when my own dearest wish was to make my absent mother notice and be proud of me, on one of her infrequent visits to the home I shared with my grandmother and my sisters? Long gone now, of course, my grandmother, my mother and all my sisters too, apart from one. Where she is I have no knowing – she may also have come to her final day, although I do not think so. I felt all the others pass, but – not her. Not yet.

But I – I see now that my last work shall be Aillean Ó Laoghaire's quilt, and I must make it my masterpiece, my swan song. I cannot see the manner of my passing, but I know that it will be soon, here, in this tiny outpost of nowhere.

And despite myself, something in me rails at that – the idea that my vast knowledge, my experience and my rare skill should be lost here, where no one of consequence will mark it.

Then again – I have spent my long life journeying between outposts of nowhere, stopping for a few days here, a se'enight there. It is fitting that I should end in one. And of course, nothing ever really comes to an end. I will go on, and Aillean will get what she wants, although perhaps not in the way she wants it.

Her quilt – my quilt too, now – will see to that.

15

The weather had taken a definite turn for the worse as Aillean closed the barn door behind her. At some point the heavy fat snowflakes that had been starting to fall as she arrived had turned into small shards of ice, disgorged from the low clouds and driven by a rising wind that set the trees to complaining and shuddering. The ice crystals had collected against walls in low drifts and made walking on the path more treacherous than it had been, and she soon realised she would make much slower progress on the homeward journey than she had on the outward leg.

She tugged her collar up and her hat down, trying to cover as much skin as possible. The wind was insistent, nipping at her clothing and driving small freezing flakes against her exposed cheeks. It tried to undo the lacings on her boots and mittens, and drove itself against her body as she pushed forward through the glittering falls of crystals. Before many minutes had passed she was chilled to the bone.

She was unable to see far ahead of her through the roiling flurries, so she tucked her head down and concentrated on following the path as it unrolled beneath her booted feet. Although it was not yet nightfall the day was dark, made shorter by the heavy clouds and the weak winter sunlight that was unable to penetrate the thick layer of airborne ice blanketing the land.

Eventually the rhythm of walking started to warm her, and she pulled up her scarf to cover her nose and mouth in an effort to thaw the skin on her cheeks. The backpack on her back bounced and sloshed reassuringly, the remaining tea in her mother's flask a temptation to stop and take refreshment. However, she was ice-born and bred; she knew that her priority was to keep moving and seek shelter as fast as she could, so she pushed on through the storm.

The journey home was lonely, dark and cold. Her breath froze on the thick woollen scarf bound across her nose, mouth and chin, leaving only her eyes exposed to the frigid wind. A crust of ice built up around the fur lining of her hood and formed crystals on her eyelashes, crackling and splintering as she moved. The wind tugged at her clothes, trying to find a way in, and ice somehow worked its way down the inside of her left boot and then melted, chilling her foot and turning it numb despite her brisk pace. She was thankful the way was not long, else she would have begun to worry about losing skin to the bite.

She arrived home just before full dark, although the snowclouds had settled low over the land and turned day into night long before sunset. Her mother looked questioningly at her as she swung the pack from her back and set it on the table, but she frowned and shook her head, and Dearbhail did not pursue it. She rested her hand on Aillean's shoulder for a moment, saying nothing, and then turned back to her preparations for the family supper.

In the next couple of hours the blizzard closed in properly, and Dearbhail would not let Cormac's trio of apprentices set off for home in the howling dark. Instead Cormac shepherded them inside the house and the three of them sat awkwardly in the kitchen, steaming gently in the heat from the range and making the room seem smaller by their presence.

The eldest, Baoth, was sixteen, approaching the end of his apprenticeship and working on his journeyman piece.

He was the most comfortable with the family, having spent a number of winter nights on makeshift beds in Dearbhail's kitchen over the course of his time with Cormac; he chatted with Dearbhail and played a game with Myrddin, Dearbhail's black cat. The two younger lads, Tanaí and Fial, aged fourteen and thirteen, were more ill at ease; Fial kept writhing his hands in his lap and fretting about whether his mother would worry about him, while Tanaí simply sat wide-eyed and watched Dearbhail and the girls as they busied themselves with the final preparations for the meal. He was a handsome lad, his black hair falling in an unruly mop over pale skin and deep green eyes, and he seemed especially interested in watching Aillean. Marthe noticed this and informed Aillean in a loud whisper, making both her and Tanaí blush awkwardly.

That night in the Ó Laoghaires' cottage was warm and cosy. There was laughter, plenty of hearty food, and a holiday feel brought by shared adversity and the presence of guests in the house. Dearbhail sewed calmly while the young folk played a complicated card game, and later Cormac brought out his harp and played a few reels while Marthe danced. As the hearthfire burned low there was storytelling to the wailing accompaniment of the storm outside, and the family and their guests went to their beds contented and warm.

16

The next morning the storm had abated somewhat, leaving brighter skies in its wake, but the prowling wind still carried occasional flurries of ice and snow. The night had been wild and there was some destruction to trees and buildings, with more that would no doubt become apparent as the snow and ice cleared in the warmer weather to come.

Cormac was out early, forcing the front door open against a drift of windblown snow and clearing a path across the yard before stoking his forge fire and checking on the family's animals. Aillean milked the goats, and then watched as the apprentice boys put away enormous quantities of breakfast against the cold and the hard work they knew would await them in the forge.

Still Aillean had not spoken to her mother about her visit to the Cailleach. There had not been the opportunity; since her arrival through the gathering storm the night before there had been no peace or private time in the house, for any of the family. If she was honest, though, Aillean knew she had kept her encounter with the Cailleach to herself partly because she was slightly ashamed of her precipitous and rather petulant exit, but also because she recognised that she did not really understand much that the woman had said to her. She did not know how to report the conversation to her mother when she was not sure she could articulate it to herself; she was not entirely sure whether the Cailleach had promised to work an enchantment into her quilt or not, and she felt certain that Dearbhail would not approve of Ríona's talk of somehow leaching Aillean's presence and personality out of the quilt and using it for her own purposes. So, to avoid the issue, she kept her silence and busied herself with chores which for the most part kept her out of Dearbhail's way.

Throughout that day, however, although she managed to avoid speaking about the Cailleach, the old woman was never far from her thoughts. She resolved to go again to visit the Maoilfhinns' barn on the morrow, and to take more food and perhaps a small gift of precious fabric from her own meagre collection, mostly donated by Dearbhail but with one or two pieces brought by her father or given by other relatives or friends. She had an aching feeling that she needed somehow to make amends, and felt much better in her own mind when she had made the firm decision to go again.

That night, however, the weather closed in once more. The apprentices had left to walk to their homes well before dusk, packed off by Dearbhail with food parcels and extra layers of clothing against the gathering cold. The family hunkered down in their warm kitchen to wait out the storm; Myrddin the cat prowled around the room elbowing and kneading until he had found the warmest spot, on Cormac's lap as he sat by the hearthfire, and then settled down with little apparent intention of moving until the snows had gone. Dearbhail got out a heavy bedspread which needed repairing and sat with it tucked over her knees while she worked on it, and the girls took turns leaning on the range or lolling on the floor wrapped in quilts or blankets.

That night was warm and cosy, but the next day, when the storm still raged, was less pleasant. The apprentices did not come and everyone was starting to get bored of each other's company, but Dearbhail expressly forbade any of them to venture further than the livestock sheds or the forge at the other side of the yard. As she said, "If I can't see the other side of the road when I look out the window, I'm not sending any of ye out onto it."

So they all sat and waited for the storm to abate. Cormac kept the forge alive and Aillean spent some time in the shed with him, partly to escape from the confines of the house and the increasingly irritable Marthe, but partly also because she had always loved her father's workspace. The golden-hot glow of the forge fire, the hiss of steam as heated metal met cooling water, the tap and chink of hammers on anvils – all these were the background noises of peace and security for her, and she was calmed by spending time in that dark warm environment.

The winter's last bombardment lasted through that day and into the next night, but by the following morning, the third since Aillean had seen the Cailleach, it had abated, leaving fresh blue skies and scudding white clouds. The temperature outside was still bitingly cold, but the wind had dropped and the bright sunlight lent the atmosphere a springlike quality.

The Ó Laoghaires all ventured outside, blinking in the dazzling brightness like moles newly emerged from their tunnels, and Cormac began to inspect the house for damage while Dearbhail made a tour of the orchard and small kitchen garden to see what had survived. The girls followed her for a while, but soon got distracted by trying to shower each other in snow by knocking it off the trees.

They were still racing around the orchard like puppies turned outside for the first time when they heard voices coming from the yard. Instantly curious, they both hurtled for the gate, skidding around and through it in a tangle of limbs and a flurry of ice crystals shed from their hair and clothes. They staggered to a halt, red-cheeked and laughing, to find their mother talking to Muireann Ó Grádaigh,

Neasa's mother. The woman was herself flushed and panting, as if she had hurried through the frigid morning to reach them. Under her arm was a package wrapped in sacking and oilskin and tied with a length of black cord.

"…completely gone," Muireann was saying. "There's naught left but a pile of rocks and the woman's body under it, all surrounded by fallen beams, covered in snow and laid out like she was on her bier. They're saying 'twas the weight of the snow made the roof collapse, and brought the walls with it."

Dearbhail had her hands to her face, horror warring with grief and shock. Aillean felt her body flush, and then go cold. She took a step forward.

"What—" she began, but then stopped, suddenly afraid of what she might hear. Dearbhail moved to put an arm around her shoulders, reaching for Marthe as well so that she stood flanked by and embracing both her daughters.

"Daughters, the Cailleach is..." She paused, searching for words, and then shook her head and threw the other woman a desperate look. "Muireann, are you sure? Is there no way she…"

Muireann was shaking her head. "No, Dearbhail. There's no doubt. Girls, there was a collapse last night in the Maoilfhinns' barn, as the storm was dying. No one heard anything through the wind until it was too late; the Cailleach was inside, and she did not come out. The barn is gone, and the Cailleach with it."

Aillean heard Muireann's words, and was still trying to process them when she felt her mother's knees begin to buckle. Dearbhail staggered and might have fallen to the icy ground but for her daughters, one on each side of her and holding her upright. She gasped and caught her breath, hauling herself erect again but retaining her grip on her daughters.

"No … she can't be … what about her frame?"

Muireann shook her head. "Went with her, broken to splinters by the wall falling on it. Nothing came out of that barn but the owl that lived in the roof. Except…" She took the parcel from under her arm and held it out. "They found this, wrapped and half buried in a snowdrift outside the door. Áine opened it, but it does not belong to her. Girl, it's your quilt."

She was looking at Aillean as she spoke, holding the parcel in front of her. For a moment no one moved, but then Dearbhail gave Aillean a small shove.

"Your quilt, girl. She must have finished it."

Haltingly Aillean moved forward a half-step and then another, until by reaching out she could touch the outer wrappings of the parcel. She did not take it, simply laying her fingers gently on its cold surface and then withdrawing them again.

Muireann was watching her. "The Cailleach's last quilt, girl. She gave Áine's back days ago, but Áine said she was still working on yours last evening when they took her bread and meat. She must have done with it in the night – but then why would she put it outside the door into the snow? It makes no sense." She shook her head in bewilderment.

Aillean whispered something, making Muireann lean forward. "Again, girl? What did you say?"

Louder, Aillean repeated her words. "She knew." She frowned. "She must have. She said to me, when I saw her, that she would finish my quilt in three days but that we would not meet again. I thought she meant she would move on early in the morning, before I came back to the village. But she knew. That's why she left my quilt outside, so it would not be buried and spoiled."

Muireann tilted her head. "But how could she have known the barn would collapse? That barn has stood since old Oillín Maoilfhinn's time, Cairell's great grandda. There's been more snow on that roof than it had on it last night, and it's held through stronger winds, too."

Aillean shrugged. "I don't know. But she did." She finally reached out and grasped the parcel, hugging it close as Muireann released it, her hands following it so that for a few seconds they were stretched out towards Aillean. For a moment they stood, the four of them, in a frozen tableau – Marthe supporting her mother, Aillean cradling the parcel containing her quilt as if it were a child, and Muireann with her arms forward and her palms facing upward as if in supplication.

Then Aillean moved, and the moment was broken. She turned away, looking down at the bundle in her arms. As she turned she spoke softly, as if to herself.

"I was going to go and see her yesterday, but I couldn't because of the snow. She knew I wouldn't, though." She began to move away, her feet carrying her towards the house in an automatic search for warmth and security. Muireann took a few following steps without thinking, but then caught herself and turned back to Dearbhail and Marthe.

Aillean's mother was still reeling from shock, but she had recovered sufficiently to say, "Muireann, you've walked a long way to bring us these tidings. Will ye step inside to warm your bones?"

Muireann hesitated. She seemed torn, wanting to be among the first to see the Cailleach's final quilt when it was unveiled by Aillean, but also knowing that the family should have this moment alone together. After a few moments of indecision her good manners won over her natural curiosity.

"No, Dearbhail, but I thank ye. I'm heading onward to the Ó Caisides' farm – I've some eggs and flour to pick up."

Dearbhail nodded, and did not press the other woman. "Aye, we're running low ourselves after yon storm. Perhaps we'll see you on your way back?"

"Aye, perhaps," Muireann agreed. She stepped forward to wrap her arms about Dearbhail's shoulders, a quick but warm embrace. The two women held each other for a moment and then stepped back, both standing taller. Muireann nodded once and then turned on her heel, heading out of the yard and back onto the slippery ice-packed roadway. Dearbhail watched her go, and then she and Marthe followed Aillean inside the house.

When they got indoors, however, Aillean was nowhere to be seen. Her boots lay discarded by the door and her oilskin overcloak was thrown over a chair, slowly dripping snowmelt onto the floor. The door to the bedroom she shared with Marthe was pointedly, determinedly closed.

On the other side of that door, Aillean was sitting on her bed staring at the fabric package as it lay on the bedspread in front of her. She did not feel grief for the Cailleach – she had not known her well or long enough for that. She did feel an automatic horror at the manner in which the woman had met her end – crushed by the collapse of a frozen building – but she did not lie to herself and pretend that she grieved.

She did, however, experience a sort of guilt, that she hadn't visited the woman as she had intended. In her rational mind she knew that the simple fact of a visit from her would not, could not possibly have altered the events of the previous night. She knew that. She also knew, though, that she had parted from the Cailleach with harsh words and a show of temper that she had already begun to feel ashamed of, even before the news of the woman's death. She wished she had been able to put that right.

She took a deep breath and held it for a moment, before puffing it out again and reaching for the parcel. Her hands shook slightly as she began to untie the black cord that bound it closed; snow had worked its way in among the threads as the package had lain outside during the night, and although much of it had fallen out or melted during its journey with Muireann, enough still remained that the cord was stiff and cold. She picked at the knots for what seemed like an age before they finally began to work loose.

Gradually she worked the loops through each other, concentrating on untying each knot instead of pulling the cord off sideways. Eventually she slipped the last end through the last loop and the cord slithered to the floor, leaving the fabric- and oilskin-wrapped parcel on the bed.

Fingers trembling in earnest now, she leaned over to pull off the first layer of wrapping. Concentrating on each fold in the sackcloth, each tuck of the oilskin, she carefully unwrapped the bundle inside, tantalised by glimpses of rich deep colours as she turned and twisted the parcel in her hands.

As she removed more of the outer wrapping the quilt began to spill out onto the bed, glowing and shimmering as it tumbled beneath her hands. Finally, curious and impatient, she gave one last pull and the remaining piece of sacking came away, allowing her quilt to unroll itself in front of her.

And it was astonishing. The Cailleach had taken her quilt, with all its imperfections and mistakes, and turned it into a piece of magic fit for royalty. The colours of the fabric patches seemed somehow to pulse, throbbing with their own rich deep life as they worked with and against their neighbours to contribute to the shifting play of colours across the quilt. As she had been before, Aillean was involuntarily pulled into one or two abiding memories as the familiar patterns of the different fabrics spoke to her in a deep, visceral language.

Then, in a throbbing instant of time that punched like one of her father's lump-hammers and left her breathless and choking, she took in the quilting.

The Cailleach had chosen a rich, thick, shimmering silvery thread for the stitches, the like of which Aillean had never seen before. It seemed to change colour to contrast with the fabric pieces it was set against, showing in some places an iridescent green, in other a startling blue and in still others a pearlescent red. Against yet other patches it showed up as bright yellow or gold, and in a few it throbbed deep and dark, the same indigo purple as the Cailleach's eyes. In the pale cream border it appeared a deep smoky grey. Everywhere, however, it was shot through with sparkling silver, which seemed to wash and glimmer like moonlight on a bubbling brook. It defied description or explanation, changing colour sometimes from one stitch to the next without a noticeable break, or gradually fading from one colour to another over the course of a loop, or a swirl, or a line of stitching.

The stitches themselves were perfect, even, and minutely tiny. They flowed and danced across the surface of the quilt, describing loops, whorls, coils, feathers, ripples, spirals as they went. Areas of the quilt were stitched with different patterns, which seemed to shift from one to the next with no apparent or obvious breaks or joins. Transitions between them were, like the changes between colours, seamless and organic; the forms and shades seemed to evolve from each other, twisting and dancing and never quite settling into predictability and order.

Some areas were loosely quilted, the lines of stitching leaving puffs of soft fabric between them. In other places, however, the quilting was heavy and intricate, stitches seeming to run into each other and create areas of dense texture. In fact, as Aillean looked closer, she realised that some – no, all – of these densely quilted areas contained images stitched in their depths – pictorial patterns that defied close examination, seeming to shift and blur as they were examined, but which somehow leaped into focus in her peripheral vision as she moved her eyes away.

In one she was sure she saw a woman, bent and burdened by a huge pack on her back, trudging along a lonely road in an area of desolate windswept moorland. In another a crowd of people gathered, clamouring for attention with their mouths open like baby birds. In a third, a smaller group of people, all women, stood calmly and looked steadily into the eyes of the observer.

There were many more areas like this, but Aillean was unsettled by the shifting textures. She stopped trying to view them, and instead she turned the quilt over to look at the backing. Again, she gasped.

For backing fabric the Cailleach had used her patchwork overskirt. Cleverly cut and stitched back together, the garment now formed a single flat piece of patchwork the same size as the front of the quilt. The last time Aillean had seen it, worn by the Cailleach herself, the fabric had been densely quilted in a dark thread; now, all that quilting had been unpicked, to be replaced with the reverse of the patterns on the other side of Aillean's quilt.

On these fabrics, however the thread shone a bright, dazzling silver, with none of the shifts or variations in colour that were apparent on the other side. In the densely quilted areas the stitches were almost too bright to look at, glittering and sparking with a fierce intensity. The odd, half-formed images were even less clear here through the crackling moonfire of the thread, but the more loosely-spaced abstract areas glimmered and flowed like drifts of stars.

The tiny scraps of fabric that made up the patchwork of the backing were in some places so worn that they were held together by the quilting, but in other places they guided its form, the colours, shapes and patterns of the tiny crumbs of material defining and ordering the patterns of stitches in ways that were not apparent from the other side. Here a piece of fabric was framed, there a particular colour was outlined, and over there a pattern was picked up and echoed in the quilting stitches. The patchwork overskirt delineated the quilting completely, driving the pattern choice and the form of the quilting.

And yet... Bewildered, Aillean flipped the quilt over again. On this side too the fabrics seemed to define the quilting, with the added dimension of the vibrant colours of the thread shooting through the whole. Patterns in the fabric were picked out and echoed, colours were matched, motifs were chosen and repeated. Somehow the organic flow of the stitching was ordered and appropriate on both sides of the quilt, although the two pieces of patchwork were very different in form and design. Aillean shook her head, astonished and humbled by the level of workmanship and creative skill laid out before her.

The quilt edges were bound in a deep but plain silver grey, chosen to match the colour assumed by the quilting thread in the cream border. Aillean ran her fingers over the binding fabric and realised that it was lightly textured, the warp and weft slightly raised in slubs and bumps. As her fingers brushed against it she heard the soft whispering sound of raw silk.

The binding was stitched down in the same silver grey thread as had been used for the quilting, although for this part of the quilt the stitches were almost invisible, except at the corners where the binding turned and mitred. There, the occasional flash or spark of silver could be seen as the fabric moved and caught the light.

Aillean caught the quilt up in her hands and ran it between them, stroking it gently and brushing it against her cheek. She pressed it against her nose and inhaled deeply. It smelled of herself, her room and the family home, but also of cold, the bitter winter outdoors, and a lingering scent of hay dust Underlying all these, however, she detected a trace of something odd and floral. This scent reminded her at once of every season of the year – the spring, with its wreaths of apple blossom and death-scented may, the summer, with its heavily scented drifts of gaudy blooms, the autumn, with the sharp-sweet odour of apples and blackberries, and the winter, with the bitter scent of pine sap and the spices of the Darknight celebration. She inhaled again, drinking in the complex aroma. Closing her eyes and falling onto the bed, she pulled the quilt over her and lost herself in the deep and hypnotic rhythm of the magic left behind by the Cailleach.

17

A long time later, or perhaps it was only a few minutes, her mother found her wrapped in the astonishing quilt, deeply asleep. Dearbhail did not disturb her daughter, simply reaching out and laying her fingers gently on the Cailleach's intricate work for a brief moment before leaving the room, pulling the door closed behind her and sending Marthe outside to keep the noise level down.

Aillean slept until early afternoon; the rest of the family ate their noon meal in near silence at Dearbhail's insistence. "The girl needs to rest," was all she would say, and Marthe and Cormac had to be content with that. In truth the atmosphere around the table was subdued anyway because of the news of the Cailleach's death, and after they had eaten Cormac set off to the village to see if he could be of any use in the clear-up that would follow once the initial shock had passed.

Aillean eventually woke and joined her mother and sister in the kitchen, bringing the quilt with her. Together they marvelled at the stitching, the thread, the colours, the workmanship; Aillean found she was protective of the piece, her quilt, but she managed to let Marthe touch it, and Dearbhail was reverent, exclaiming softly under her breath and marvelling at the astonishing craftsmanship. Even Cormac, when he returned from the village, tired, aching and in sombre mood, was moved to comment that he'd never seen anything like it.

"Sure, girl, that's not your work? Not the same quilt ye took with ye, all wrapped in old sack cloth? She worked a wonder on it, that's for certain. Tis a thing of beauty indeed." He reached out to run his calloused workman's fingers over the iridescent stitches. "Too good for the likes of me, and that's a fact."

Aillean shook her head. "No, Da. It's not too good for you – it's got you in it. Look, there, see? There's a patch from your old work breeches. And there, your old scarf, and there the nightshirt you wore until Mam hid it and cut it up without you knowing." She pointed.

Cormac squinted, and then shook his head in helpless wonder. "You're right, girl, but those clothes surely did not look as fine on me as they do in this wondrous piece o' magic."

Marthe was crowding close. "Am I in it too?"

Aillean gave her a scornful look. "Of course you are – you know it, you sat next to me for most of the hours I was making it. You're there, look – there's your skirt, the one you wore to the Longday picnic last year and then tore on thorns when you were climbing that may tree. And there's a baby dress we both wore – see, that one there?"

Marthe peered. "Yes – and there's my doll's dress, that I didn't want after I lost the doll. And there's Mam's old apron, and a piece from the quilt that used to be on our bed, and – that's Grandma's old blanket, isn't it?" She grinned with delight. "We're all in here! All except Myrddin." She picked up the cat and hugged him to her.

Aillean chuckled. "He sat on my lap while I was sewing and stuck his claws in it, so he's there too. But…" She paused, furrowing her brow. "The Cailleach is here too, in the quilting. I think she put herself in it, somehow. She's in the patterns in the quilting, and in the thread, and the pictures."

Dearbhail was rubbing the quilt between forefinger and thumb, feeling the texture of the fabrics and the stitches. She nodded absently.

"Aye, child, she is that. I've never seen quilting like this, nor thread neither. She has given you a great gift. But – what pictures do you mean? There's only the quilting patterns, no pictures."

Aillean reached over and pointed to one of the most densely quilted sections, where she had seen the image of the woman struggling along a lonely road bowed and burdened by her heavy pack. "There, see? If you kind of look sideways at the stitches, instead of straight on, there's a picture in them."

Dearbhail squinted at the place where Aillean was pointing. "I can't see it, girl. Where do you mean?"

"There, Mam. Right where my finger is – see? There's a woman, walking along a road with a huge load on her. I think it's supposed to be the Cailleach, walking between villages with her quilting frame on her back."

Dearbhail frowned and looked closer, but then drew back shaking her head. "Child, there's nothing, just the stitches. It's closely quilted, to be sure, but there's no picture."

Marthe pushed forward. "Let me see, Mam. Maybe it's your eyes." Dearbhail spluttered in protest, but Marthe took no notice, leaning forward to see the area that Aillean had indicated.

After a few seconds she too drew back. "Aillean, it's not Mam's eyes, it's yours. There's nothing there, just a load of stitches."

It was Aillean's turn to frown. Pushing Marthe out of the way she focused on the area of stitching, narrowing her eyes.

"Yes! It is there, but you have to sort of look to the side of it. If you don't look straight at it, you can see it. Here, look, there's another one, of the Cailleach's frame all set up. See?"

Marthe and Dearbhail both squinted and peered, and even Cormac came to have a look, tilting his head to look carefully where Aillean indicated. In the end, however, they all admitted that they could see nothing, only the Cailleach's intricate network of stitches.

Aillean was baffled. To her eyes the images were clearly present – not clear to see, because of the curious blurring and shifting if she tried to view them straight on, but they were certainly there if she let them appear in her peripheral vision. In the end she concluded that her family were looking at them too closely, or too directly, or something. She could see them, but they could not – she did not understand it, but then she understood little of what the Cailleach had said or done, and she supposed this oddity, and the fact that even she had to creep up on the images in order to see them, must be some part of the old woman's enchantment.

Later, snatching a few more stolen moments in her room while dinner preparation went on beyond the closed door, she turned the quilt over to its reverse side and searched for the images again. Every time she tried to count them she came up with a different number, but after a few attempts she decided that there were either eleven or twelve, all depicting scenes from what she supposed must be the Cailleach's life. In one she was a child, but still recognisable as the Cailleach by the patchwork skirt she wore. The child held a needle and thread in one hand, but was wailing and holding up the other hand to show a small wound weeping blood. Aillean grinned ruefully, and not without sympathy; it seemed the Cailleach had not always been an expert needleworker.

Another showed two women, both wearing the patchwork skirt of a Cailleach, but one young, standing straight and tall, and the other twisted, bent and old beyond imagining, lying on a bed. The ancient crone was handing the young woman a bundle, which was spilling open at one side to reveal a quilt folded within. In yet another the young woman was sitting bent over the assembled quilting frame and working on a quilt.

There were others, all depicting scenes from one woman's long life. In the final one, which Aillean could sometimes find, sometimes not, the woman was standing outside a barn that looked very much like the Maoilfhinns'. She was gazing directly out of the image and her eyes somehow seemed to follow Aillean as she moved, never mind that the image was invisible unless viewed from the side, and not always then.

Finally, after squinting at the stiches for long enough to make her eyes ache, she shook her head in exasperation. Standing, she folded the quilt and placed it carefully at the end of her bed.

Stepping back she looked down at it. It was now too beautiful a thing for everyday use, but its construction was also a part of her everyday life. To be truthful, she was not sure what use the piece might ever have; it was ornate, astonishing and sacred, and yet somehow still workaday and practical. She felt instinctively the deep contradiction that it should be cared for with great reverence, but also touched, handled and used.

As she gazed at it she drew in a shallow breath, held it for a few seconds and then released it. She laid her hand gently on the quilt's surface, across a red and brown patch from one of her mother's old dresses juxtaposing one from a deep blue shawl of her grandmother's. Almost without thinking she spoke, breathing the words into the silence of her room.

"Thank you."

18

You are welcome, girl. Although whether you will thank me when your time comes to leave home and take to the road, I do not know. I certainly did not thank my mother, the long-ago Cailleach who passed her gift on to me all that time ago.

For, girl, that is what you are now. The mystery is passed, sometimes from mother to daughter, sometimes between sisters, and sometimes between strangers as I have passed it to you. My mother passed it to me, and to all her daughters – unusual, that, for a single Cailleach to give her gift to more than one woman. All gone now, though, apart from Ainnir, and where she is I do not know. But I have not felt her pass, so I can hope that she felt my departure from this world and spared me a thought.

I am not conscious, in the usual sense of the word; I am simply the ghost of a breath stitched into the warp and weft of your quilt. I had thought to use its raw emotion, its deep sense of home and family to heal my failing body and remake myself for another few tens of years on the road. The Hag had other ideas, however, and the knowledge of my time came upon me with a finality that I could not struggle against.

In truth, I did not wish to; my lifetime has been far too long. But here, at the end, I grieve for you, girl, whose family means more to you than you know. Your precocious and cocky sister, your capable and emotional mother, your handsome father with his boundless love wrapping all his womenfolk in its safe embrace – all these things you will, eventually, have to leave behind.

In the end, the mystery will see to that, and the quilt that is all I was and all you are and will be. It will pass on the magic, and it will push, tug, prise you from your home, drive you to set out along the cold lonely road with only a quilting frame and a small stock of threads and fabrics to your name.

During the years, as you grow, the quilt will make you want to sew, will drive you to work harder, be better, sew a more perfect seam. And it will help you to become more capable, guiding your fingers until the work becomes automatic and skilled, so that you can move beyond the mechanics of stitching to become truly creative. The stitches will flow, and you will start to develop a reputation for expertise and skill beyond the level of those around you.

You will begin to feel the quilts you work on, whether they are your own, your mother's, your sister's or a stranger's, a woman from the next village or a distant farm who has heard of your uncommon ability and arrived at your home with a bundle under one arm, begging you to work on it in return for food, money, fabric. You will know what the maker desires, but beyond that you will somehow know what the woman truly needs, and with time you will start to feel how to stitch those needs into the quilts. This is the mystery.

When the recognition comes, you will fight it. You will know in your heart what you are, but you will not know what to do about it. Everything in you will rebel against the notion that you must leave, must travel and take your gift with you, but you will be driven to it, made anxious and angry and unable to settle until you accept the inevitable. The mystery will not let you rest in one place. This I discovered through many years of trying.

Your father will make your frame for you, once it becomes clear to you what you are, so that you will carry some of his own fierce and protective enchantment with you at least as long as that frame lasts. When you wear it out, however – and you will wear it out, over years and years of use – you will be on your own, as I am. Was.

You will travel at first in a small circuit around your home, returning frequently, but soon you will range further and return less often, staying away first for months and then for years at a time. Your family will age without you; you will not be there when your mother passes, nor your father. You will not see the growing up of your sister's children – they will know you only as a distant, occasional and mysterious presence, who turns up at irregular intervals and causes their mother, your sister, to weep long into the night when you leave again.

You will not wed – you will never stay in one place long enough for that. You may bear children, the result of careless assignations with handsome men in the towns and villages you pass through, but you will not rear them – you will know that your life is no life for a mother, so you will leave the babes with their fathers, or perhaps with an aunt or grandmother. Perhaps you might even return to your own mother or sister, leaving your little ones with them as a lasting reminder that you were once part of their family – as my mother did with me and my sisters.

You will travel on, working your magic on every quilt you can. You will stay for a few days, maybe a se'enight in each place, always moving on before people become comfortable with your presence. Your mystery must be maintained – soon you will realise that, and you will work hard to build and keep it. When your health begins to fail, the years on the road taking their toll, you will understand that you can renew yourself by drawing life and vitality from a quilt in the way I planned to use yours, before the knowledge of my time came upon me.

You may meet other Cailleachs – we are a dwindling sisterhood, sometimes falling to natural attrition or accident, but it is also true that some of us choose not to pass on the mystery when we end our days, so there are fewer of us each year.

There are some left, though, treading their seasonal rounds, and when Cailleachs meet there is a circling, like two cats unsure of one other. There may be some hissing, perhaps some spitting, and occasionally fur will fly, but usually after a time the hackles will be laid flat and we will spend a companionable time together before going our solitary ways. There is no passing of lore or technique – each Cailleach works her mystery according to her own skills – but there is fellow feeling, and word is passed of which roads are safe, which villages or taverns may be suitable places to lodge or bide a while, and which should be avoided.

In the end, though, you will be truly alone. Friends and family grow, live, die. Houses, farms and inns change hands or fall to ruin, forests are cut down and regrow, rivers change their course, but you will endure, sustained by your magic and renewing yourself over and again until suddenly, with a shocking, inevitable but ultimately welcome finality, your end will be upon you.

There, at the last, you will make the choice that I did. If you have a female descendent who wishes it, the gift will be given easily – my mother was able to pass her skill to all her daughters, although that is a rare thing. Or if there is a girl who presents herself at that critical moment, a girl who might one day have the makings of a Cailleach, you may decide to pass on the gift and the burden to her – as I did with you. If there is no such girl, or if you choose not to, your mystery will die with you.

I cannot say, now, why I chose to burden you, Aillean Ó Laoghaire. Perhaps I felt that you would be able to survive the rigours of the life I have condemned you to. Maybe it was that when I asked you for your heart's desire to be stitched into your quilt, you simply asked to be able to sew. Perhaps I merely panicked at the thought of my decades, centuries of experience being lost, and I settled on you because your quilt sparked my interest at a vital moment. Whichever – you are chosen, and you will have no alternative other than to follow the path I have laid out for you.

May the gods grant you luck, strength, and the grace to remember me with something other than resentment.

Acknowledgements

As always, no book is ever written by the author alone. Many people have been part of this story, and thanks are due to all.

To dear friends who have been my cheerleaders along the way – you all know who you are. Thank you.

To my generous and diligent early readers – Ruth, Tom, Caitlin. You made the story better, and any problems that remain are my responsibility, not yours.

To my internet people – if we're connected via email or on the socials and we've chatted about writing, stories or life, you're part of this too.

Finally, to my family: my mother and grandmothers, for teaching me to sew; Ellen and Lizzie, for not allowing any of my bullshit; Molly, Owen and Caitlin, for reading and encouragement; and Tom, for company, endless cups of tea, unfailing enthusiasm for my work, and for not complaining when I need to go off on my own to do words. Love you all.

Louise Maskill is a freelance author and editor. She lives in Derbyshire in the UK surrounded by cats, books and apple trees, but one day she will migrate north. She has published non-fiction in a variety of genres, but her first love is writing fiction. *Cailleach* is her first self-published novel.

Find Louise online at her website:
https://lmaskill.com
or search for her by name on Instagram,
Facebook, Threads, Goodreads and Amazon.

You can email her at:
louise@lmaskill.com

For regular updates about forthcoming titles,
subscribe to her mailing list at:
https://lmaskill.com/mailinglist

Hagthorn
Press

Printed in Great Britain
by Amazon

38908269R00078